CW00643396

I KNOCKED UP
SATAN'S
DAUGHTER

Also by Carlton Mellick III

Satan Burger
Electric Jesus Corpse
Sunset With a Beard (stories)
Razor Wire Pubic Hair
Teeth and Tongue Landscape
The Steel Breakfast Era
The Baby Jesus Butt Plug
Fishy-fleshed
The Menstruating Mall
Ocean of Lard (with Kevin L. Donihe)
Punk Land
Sex and Death in Television Town
Sea of the Patchwork Cats
The Haunted Vagina
Cancer-cute (Avant Punk Army Exclusive)
War Slut
Sausagey Santa
Ugly Heaven
Adolf in Wonderland
Ultra Fuckers
Cybernetrix
The Egg Man
Apeshit
The Faggiest Vampire
The Cannibals of Candyland
Warrior Wolf Women of the Wasteland
The Kobold Wizard's Dildo of Enlightenment +2
Zombies and Shit
Crab Town
The Morbidly Obese Ninja
Barbarian Beast Bitches of the Badlands
Fantastic Orgy (stories)

I KNOCKED UP SATAN'S DAUGHTER

CARLTON MELLICK III

ERASERHEAD PRESS
PORTLAND, OREGON

ERASERHEAD PRESS
205 NE BRYANT
PORTLAND, OR 97211

WWW.ERASERHEADPRESS.COM

ISBN: 1-936383-82-9

AUTHOR'S NOTE

This book is a romantic comedy. Yeah, that's right, I wrote a fucking romantic comedy. You got a problem with that? You think you're too cool for romantic comedies or something? Well, maybe I like romantic comedies. No matter how stupid and formulaic they all are, it's impossible to stop watching the damned things until the two main characters get together in the end. Let me make this clear: I don't ever watch these movies on purpose. Hell no. But, you know, sometimes I just find myself in a room while somebody else is watching one and then I get sucked in. I can't help it. Have you watched all of those Ben Stiller rom-coms? I want to punch that guy in the face and, yet, I still won't turn the damn television off if one of his movies comes on.

It has been a running joke in the bizarro fiction scene for a while now. Who was going to be the first to write a bizarro romantic comedy? Well, after I came up with the idea of a guy who gets forced into marrying a succubus after he unintentionally knocks her up (which probably came to my mind while I was watching the anime *My Bride is a Mermaid*) I decided it was going to be me. I approached the story exactly as if I were writing a Hollywood rom-com, right down to following the romantic comedy 7-point formula that you've probably seen a gazillion times before. Of course, this story isn't your usual Adam Sandler/Drew Barrymore chick flick. It's got sex, violence, and demons and shit. That's what romantic comedies have been missing: demons and shit.

Although the reason I wrote it was kind of a joke, I fell in love with this story and really enjoyed writing the thing. It might even be one of my absolute favorites. Of course, if it ends up being the book I'm most remembered for after I die I'll be pretty pissed. I mean, even Kobold Wizard would be better and that one was retarded. But, yeah, as a writer you should be happy if you're remembered for anything at all. Because, most likely, nobody's going to remember you for shit.

By the way, if you want to see some romantic comedies that are good, and I mean *actually* good. Watch Korean romantic comedies. They are much better than anything that's come out of Hollywood… because they are actually romantic and they are actually funny. Not to mention they make you fall in love with characters who are borderline psychopaths.

So here you go: *I Knocked Up Satan's Daughter*. I hope you like it.

- Carlton Mellick III 9/3/2011 9:58 pm

PS - By the way, what the hell is up with the tagline on the back cover of this book anyway? She came for his soul, but left with his heart? Are you fucking serious? I don't even think Hollywood rom-coms have taglines that stupid.

PPS - Okay, I admit I'm really the one who came up with the tagline on the back cover. I cried when I came up with it. Shut up.

CHAPTER ONE

Jonathan Vandervoo is what most people would call a loser. His parents think he's a loser, his friends think he's a loser, his neighbors, teachers, girls, pretty much everyone he meets sees him as nothing but a pathetic waste of space. It might be the way he keeps his hair in a messy ball somewhere between a perm and dreadlocks, or the way his shaggy Goodwill suits always seem to be coated in dog hair and dead grass even though he doesn't own a dog or a lawn. It might be because he dropped out of college one credit away from graduation or because he's never been able to hold a job for more than a month. Perhaps it's because he doesn't seem to be able to shave properly, wash his clothes without shrinking them, or even tie his own shoes.

Or maybe it's because he lives in a house made of Legos.

Jonathan considers himself a master at building with Legos. He's been obsessed with them ever since he was a little kid. His parents encouraged his lego-playing when he was young; buying him all the legos he wanted, because they hoped the boy would one day grow up to be an architect like his father. They hoped the toy would influence him in this direction, and were very pleased that he spent so much time building miniature houses and cities.

"He'll be a fine hard-working Christian architect," his father always used to say, nodding proudly at his boy.

But as he got older, Jonathan never developed any interest in becoming an architect. He just wanted to keep playing with legos. Through high school, college, and into his twenties, Jonathan never stopped building things with the multi-colored blocks. And as he grew up, the size and scope of his creations also grew with him. He started building lego elephants the size of real elephants, lego Mini Coopers the size of real Mini Coopers, lego army men that stood as high as he was. He's built a lego piano, a lego chainsaw, a lego television that played an episode of Lego Two and a Half Men.

"But none of these things serve a purpose," his father always says. "Why build anything that serves no purpose?"

"Because it's fun," Jonathan always says with a big smile.

When his parents threatened to kick him out of their house unless he stopped playing with legos and got a real job, Jonathan just walked down the street to a vacant lot and built himself his own three story lego mansion. It might not have all of the luxuries of a normal house, but he's happy living there. And without needing to pay rent, he doesn't have to worry about a day job. He's free to dedicate as much time as he wants to building his lego works of art.

Perhaps most people would see him as a loser for dedicating all of his time building things with legos, but Jonathan couldn't disagree more. He believes lego-building is an important form of art that deserves just as much recognition as any other art form. And it is his goal in life to build the greatest lego creations this world has ever seen.

Jonathan wakes to the sound of knocking coming from the front door downstairs. He rolls over in his dragon-shaped lego bed and pulls the pink blanket over his eyes. The knocking continues.

He's sure it's just another customer. From 2pm to 6pm, if he happens to be at home, Jonathan opens his lego house to the public. He charges $5 per person to tour his home. This brings in about $15-35 dollars a week, which is plenty of money for him to buy food, beer, and more legos. But he has no intention of answering the door for this customer. It's only ten in the morning and he never lets anyone inside before 2pm.

After what seems like an hour of knocking, he finally gets out of bed. But before he pulls on his yellow plaid suit pants and buttons up his too-small pumpkin-orange shirt, the knocking stops. He pushes open the blue lego shutters and looks out of the window, but doesn't see anybody standing outside. The neighborhood is quiet. Everyone is at work or school. Not a single car is on the street.

Jonathan shrugs and goes about his morning routine. He takes a shower in the black and white checkered bathroom. The water comes from a small tank of rain water on the roof, and sprinkles down on him through a flower-shaped spout. The water is usually pretty cold and the supply is limited, so he always keeps his showers brief. They aren't as soothing as the hot showers he took when he lived with his parents, but he likes the feeling of the bumpy lego tiles beneath his bare feet and likes that he'll never be in danger of slipping in the tub.

After the shower is over, the excess water drains out through a pipe onto his flower garden outside. The flowers don't need to be watered, though. They too are made out of legos.

He gets dressed and goes downstairs to the kitchen on the second floor. He makes breakfast, which is the same breakfast he has every morning: toast! With his battery-powered snail-shaped lego toaster, he cooks up some scrumptious toast with honey. This is pretty much the only food Jonathan eats when he's at home. His lego oven is just a decoration and doesn't actually work, nor does his lego microwave. Only his toaster works, so it's the only hot food he can make for himself. He's perfectly fine with that, though, because he absolutely loves toast.

With honey dribbling down his cheek as he carries his breakfast in his mouth, he goes downstairs to his workshop. The entire ground floor of his lego house is one wide open room where he constructs all of his lego sculptures. Many of his works are on display for his visitors, set up like some kind of cheerful art museum. But most of the sculptures Jonathan builds do not go on display. He only has a limited number of legos, most of which were used to build his house, so he doesn't keep his creations around for long. When he builds a new piece, he displays it for about a week, takes a picture, and disassembles it. He has hundreds of photo albums full of pictures of his creations. Whenever he feels sad or lonely, all he has to do is flip through a photo album and it will always cheer him up.

He turns on his iPod to play some mariachi punk music, and then gets to work. For the past two years, Jonathan has worked while listening to mariachi punk. It's his new favorite genre of music, which was invented by a scene of urban Mexican street punks. Basically, it is pop punk with a mariachi-style horn section. It's very underground in Mexico and even more underground in other countries.

While bobbing his tangled hair to the mariachi beat, he

dives into his creation with all of his heart and soul. He builds a life-sized sculpture of a crippled devil in a wheelchair, with a long Santa beard and curly mountain ram horns. When Jonathan builds, he builds fast. Really fast. His hands move so quickly that it's as if somebody has pushed a fast forward button on his body. He can stick the legos into place flawlessly with each motion, no matter how quickly he moves. Within just a couple of hours, the new sculpture is already complete.

He stands back and admires his work. The lego devil glares up at him with an angry face. He isn't sure why he decided to give the devil such an ugly, menacing facial expression. He isn't sure why he decided to create a devil at all. Normally, he prefers to create cute things like giant smiling ladybugs and unicycle-riding geckos. But this one just creeps him out. When he rolls the wheelchair-bound devil into the display section of the room, he faces it away from him. He decides he doesn't want to look the thing in the eyes again until it's time to take him apart.

When two o'clock rolls around and it's time for the lego house to open up for visitors, Jonathan steps through the front door and breathes in the afternoon air. He flips over the closed sign, stretches like a waking cat, and then he decides to begin his next sculpture.

On his way back inside, something catches the corner of his eye. There's graffiti on the wall of his house, just next to the door. But the graffiti isn't spray-painted on his house, it is burned into the lego wall as if done with a blowtorch. The words are warped from the melted plastic, but it seems to be some kind of message.

It reads:

"You weren't home when I came by, so I'll be back later. I have a surprise for you! Hugs! Kisses!"

– Lici

There is also a heart drawn around the words, like it was intended to be some kind of love note. And next to the name Lici, there is a pair of lip prints burned into the wall, as if a girl kissed the legos with black lipstick.

Jonathan is confused by the message. He doesn't know anyone named Lici. He assumes the note couldn't possibly be for him. But he has no idea how somebody could have gotten the wrong house (because who else has a lego house?) or why the hell anyone would use a blowtorch to leave a message. Jonathan begins to get worried. Perhaps it's some crazy lego fanatic who has been lurking around his house. Or perhaps it's a pyromaniac who wants to burn his lego house down. He used to know a kid in grade school who built houses out of legos and then set them on fire to watch them burn. Jonathan hated that kid. Burning legos is one of the worst things you can possibly do. It's like burning away all hope and possibility. To Jonathan, it is blasphemy.

He goes back inside. He isn't too bothered by the vandalism—his lego house is easy to fix—but his paranoid imagination about who left the note runs wild on him. It's all that he can think about for the rest of the day.

CHAPTER TWO

"You say they burned note on your house?" Shoji asks Jonathan in his thick Japanese accent, his voice so belligerently loud that it can be heard by everyone in the bar. "You don't let them get away with this!"

Then Shoji takes a swig from a can of Hamm's.

Shoji is a five hundred pound Asian man, who is the closest thing Jonathan has to a best friend even though Jonathan can't understand him half of the time. He's also the only person over the age of ten who doesn't think Jonathan is a loser for living in a lego house. This is because Shoji knows what it feels like to be considered a loser by everyone close to him. Like Jonathan and his legos, Shoji has a passion that his family never approved of. Shoji has the desire to become a professional sumo wrestler. But nobody has ever taken his dream seriously. They all think he's an alcoholic loser. They think he should sober up, lose all the weight, go back to school, and get a real job. But Shoji refuses to abandon his dream. He promises that one day he will become Yokozuna, the grand champion of all sumos.

"It's probably nothing," Jonathan says, sitting two seats away from Shoji to accommodate his friend's massive amount of excess weight. "Just somebody messing with me."

"You want me to go down there and teach punks a lesson?" Then he raises his fists over his head and flexes his flabby muscles. "Show them my powerful sumo skills?"

Jonathan shakes his head. "No, she's probably harmless."

"She?" Shoji lowers his fists and raises an eyebrow, creating large rolls in his forehead. "A girl did this?"

"Yeah, I think so," Jonathan says. "The note had hearts and kisses on it, somehow burned into the wall."

Shoji smiles widely.

"Jonusan!" he says. Jonusan is how Shoji pronounces Jonathan's name. "Jonusan has new crazy girlfriend!" Then he laughs loudly with his head stretched all the way back, patting

Jonathan on the shoulder with such force that the young man nearly falls off of his bar stool.

"I don't have a girlfriend," Jonathan says. "I have no idea who did it."

Shoji takes a quick swig of beer and leans in close. "Jonusan, you going to go for it? You know, go for it?"

Shoji winks at him. By the look in his eyes and the unsteadiness of his head as it bobbles on his wide neck, Jonathan can tell that Shoji is already incredibly drunk. Shoji is a heavy drinker, though, and Jonathan is very used to hanging around him when he's had way too many.

"I don't think so," Jonathan says, breaking eye contact. "It's not what you think."

Shoji says, "Jonusan, when's the last time you been with a girl?"

Jonathan shrugs, staring at a row of bottles behind the bar.

Shoji yanks on Jonathan's chin so that he faces him.

"A month?" Shoji says, spitting into his face. "Five months?"

"I've never been with a woman," Jonathan says.

"Never?" Shoji says.

"I'm still a virgin," Jonathan says, whispering.

"Impossible!" Shoji says.

"I've never had sex."

Shoji points a finger at Jonathan. "Didn't I set you up with my cousin last November? You had to have done sex with her. She does sex with everybody!"

Jonathan looks down. He doesn't like to remember that night. "No, we were about to, but then she changed her mind once she saw me naked."

Shoji rubs his chin and remembers. "Oh, yeah! She said you had something wrong with your penis. What was wrong with it again?"

"My penis is all black," Jonathan says.

"Black?"

Jonathan points at a patch of black paint on the wall behind the bar. "It's pitch black, like it's been painted. Your cousin thought it was some kind of strange STD and wouldn't go near it."

"Yeah, that's it! Black penis!" Shoji laughs out loud. "Freak dicki!" When he calms his laughing, he asks, "Were you born with the penis that way? A penis birth problem?"

"No," Jonathan says. "It only happened last July. I have no idea how it happened. I just woke up one morning and it was all black. The doctors don't know what it is. They've never seen anything like it before. They guess it's just a rare skin pigmentation problem."

Shoji just laughs louder, his rolls of fat jiggling, knocking over his stack of cans across the bar. "You're a funny guy, Jonusan. Funny, funny guy."

Jonathan looks around the bar to make sure nobody heard their conversation, but he notices three frat boys staring right at him with smirks on their faces. They surely heard everything. When Jonathan locks eyes with one of them, all three of the frat guys stand up and approach.

Jonathan turns to Shoji, ignoring the frat boys as they walk to the bar. Shoji is busy restacking his beer cans into a pyramid.

"Hey," he hears one of the frat kids say to him.

Jonathan reluctantly turns to face them.

"Aren't you Chuck Vandervoo's brother?" says one frat kid, the one covered in too many freckles and muscles to count.

Chuck is Jonathan's younger, more respectable brother. He's an all-American college athlete and gun enthusiast. His father's pride and joy. While Jonathan doesn't recognize any of these kids, they seem like just the kind of guys his younger brother would be friends with.

"Yeah," Jonathan says.

"I told you it was him!" the frat boy says to his friends. They give each other high-fives and smile at Jonathan. Then they turn back to him.

"Is it true?" Freckled Frat Boy asks. "Do you really live in a house made of legos?"

"Yeah," Jonathan says.

"No shit!" the frat boy says. All three of them get excited. This, in turn, makes Jonathan excited. He loves meeting fans of his work, even though there are so few of them. They give each other another quick round of high fives.

"I've always wanted to ask you something," says Freckled Frat Boy.

"What?" Jonathan asks.

"I've always wanted to ask... " The frat boy pauses to grin. Then he says, "Are you fucking retarded or what?"

The other two frat boys burst into laughter and high five each other.

Freckled Frat Boy says, "I mean, you'd have to be retarded to actually want to live in that fucking ugly piece of shit building. Oh wait, that's right, your brother said you had to live there because your parents kicked you of their house for being an immature virgin who plays with legos all day. How fucking old are you anyway?"

Jonathan stares forward. He just plays along to get through this as quickly as possible. It's nothing new to him.

"Twenty-four," he replies.

"Then why don't you act like it?" says Freckled Frat Boy. "Why don't you get a job and move into a real house like a normal person?"

"I like my house," Jonathan says. "I would rather live there than anywhere else in the world."

"That's not what your brother said. He said that you live in that house because you're scared. You're scared of getting a job, scared of driving cars, scared of having any sort of responsibility whatsoever. It's pathetic."

Before Jonathan could respond, Shoji slams his fist onto the bar, exploding his freshly-built pyramid of beer cans.

"Enough!" Shoji yells.

Then he stands up, his enormous belly knocks over his bar stool as he stumbles to face the frat boys.

"You don't understand what it means to have a dream," Shoji says to the frat boys with his booming drunken voice. "Jonusan lives better than any of you. Unlike you, he has no worries. He don't worry about getting to shitty job on time or paying rent or getting kids to school." The frat guys giggle at each other as the enormous drunken Asian man gives his slurred speech. "Like me, Jonusan lives in ultimate happiness, because he has only one path in life. And that is to pursue his passion. You'll one day wish you were as brave as my friend, Jonusan."

Then Freckled Frat Boy says, "Sit your fat ass down, King Hippo. I wasn't talking to you."

As soon as the Freckled Frat Boy says this, Jonathan knows what is going to happen next. He's seen it happen a dozen times before.

Shoji's eyes bug angrily out of his head and his chin raises high into the air.

"You do not insult a Yokozuna," Shoji says, stumbling back and forth. "You will regret your words."

"Get the fuck out of here lard ass," says Freckled Frat Boy, "before we make bacon out of you."

The frat boys turn to walk away, not interested in a fight.

"Do you know who you insult?" Shoji yells across the bar at them, his words barely comprehensible. "I am number one sumo champion in Japan!" Then shoji pulls off his shirt to reveal his enormous breasts and belly.

As he removes his shoes and pants, the bartender says, "Shoji, I told you not to take your clothes off in here anymore."

"My sumo power will teach you the meaning of fear and respect," Shoji says, now only in his white boxer briefs hanging halfway down his ass, as he stumbles into the center of the room, facing the frat boys.

Freckled Frat Boy turns around.

"You wanna go, fat ass?" he says. "Let's go then. Muscle versus fat."

Shoji squats down into the sumo starting position. He stomps his left foot, then stomps his right foot, then throws salt across the floor to appease the Shinto gods.

"You fail to understand," Shoji says. "Sumo wrestlers are just as much muscle as they are fat. We are powerful warriors and destroy everything in path!"

Then Shoji roars at the top of his lungs and barrels forward.

"Oh shit," Freckled Frat Boy cries as he realizes there is a five hundred pound wall of meat flying toward him.

The freckled kid dives out of the way just in time, but Shoji keeps going. He sloppily plows forward, trips over his discarded shoes, and collapses, crushing a small table beneath him. The frat boys burst into laughter at the drunken sumo wrestler and then run out of the bar, high-fiving each other. When Jonathan checks to see if his friend is all right, he hears snoring coming from the wreckage. Shoji has fallen fast asleep.

The reason Shoji has never gotten anywhere in his sumo career is for one reason and one reason only: he sucks at sumo when he's drunk. And he's always, always drunk.

On his walk home, Jonathan can't get the words the frat boy said to him out of his head. The words his brother had told him, about how he lives the way he does because he's afraid of responsibility. The thing is, his brother is right. Jonathan is afraid of responsibility. He's created his life around getting out of responsibility. He lived with his parents for so many years because he didn't want to have to take care of himself. He dropped out of school because he knew that after graduating he would have to take that first step into the real world. But Jonathan is scared of the real world. He feels safer living in a world of fantasy, one that he builds for himself one colorful lego block at a time, where he never has to face the challenges that normal people have to face.

"I need to see you, Priscilla," he says, picking up the pace to get home as soon as possible. "Only your face will remove these ugly thoughts from my head."

Because he has always had problems getting a girlfriend, and was so lonely living all by himself in his house, Jonathan decided to build himself a girlfriend out of legos. Priscilla is Jonathan's prize lego creation. He keeps her in a secret upstairs room, hidden away from the public. She is too precious to share with anyone else.

When he gets home, he rushes upstairs, turning on flashlights that hang from his ceiling like light bulbs as he goes. He gets to the top floor and goes to a bright green lego wall with a rose pattern in the tiles. As he pushes the center of the rose, the wall opens up and battery-powered light fills the secret chamber. Just a brief moment of gazing into Priscilla's yellow lego face and all of Jonathan's worries completely vanish.

"I've missed you so much," Jonathan says, stepping into the room with her.

His lego girlfriend has long red hair that flows down her shoulders, beautiful blue eyes that he can gaze into for hours on end, and perky breasts that just drive Jonathan wild. She's currently wearing a blue evening gown with matching blue earrings. Jonathan makes her a new outfit every other week, but this particular dress he's made is particularly enchanting.

With alcohol in his blood enlivening his senses, he turns on his iPod to a romantic violin concerto.

"Shall we dance?" Jonathan says to Priscilla.

Then he wraps his arms around her in an embrace and they dance together. Jonathan carefully lifts her feet from the floor and attaches them to the legos on another side of the floor, then pulls her out of those legos and attaches them to another section of lego. But for some reason, their dancing feels more mechanical than it has in the past. Less magical. And for a moment, just a moment, Jonathan doesn't see her as a woman. He just sees her as a pile of lego pieces in human-form; a plastic, blocky, poor excuse for a female figure.

He quickly shakes the thought and kisses her bumpy red lips. But when he pulls away he sees a look of sadness in her deep blue eyes, as if she heard his cruel thoughts.

"I'm sorry," he says to her. "I didn't mean it."

Then he wipes tears from her cheek. He doesn't realize that the tears are falling from his own eyes.

CHAPTER THREE

Jonathan wakes in his dragon bed to the sound of knocking on his front door. His head spins as he looks at his windup clock to check the time. It's 2:30pm. He's slept in. He gags on something in the back of his throat and coughs a blue four-pronged lego into his hand. It's one of Priscilla's earrings. When he staggers out of bed, he slips on a pile of green legos. They must have broken off of his bed frame when he staggered into bed the night before. A shooting pain goes up his heel as the corners of the legos jab into his bare feet—a pain he's grown accustomed to.

He staggers downstairs toward the front door, buttoning his slobber-stained orange shirt. He could really use some customers today. Most of his money was blown at the bar last night. If the visitor is a child he hopes his parents aren't with him. Parents will smell the alcohol on him and word will get around that the lego house isn't a safe place for children.

When he opens the door, he is so relieved that there aren't children with parents that he doesn't immediately recognize what he is looking at. Standing on his porch is a woman with red skin. She's in some kind of devil costume. Horns curl out of her short black hair and a pointed demon tail whips around behind her waist like a dancing serpent.

Jonathan balances himself against the door frame and looks into her lime-green eyes. She has an explosive look of excitement on her face, smiling so wide that it seems as though it must hurt her face. The excitement appears to be overwhelming her so much that she's shaking; she opens her mouth to speak but can't seem to find any words. Then Jonathan remembers the note from yesterday and he steps back a little. He realizes this odd woman in the odd devil costume must be the same person who left the note. Judging by how excited and nervous she is, Jonathan decides his assumption was correct. She has to be some kind of crazy lego fan who was dying to meet him and tour his wonderful lego house.

For a few more minutes, she just stands there with her crazed murky-red lipstick smile. Then she lifts her white tank top and points at her belly. Jonathan didn't notice it before, but the woman's stomach is as swollen as a soccer ball.

"I'm pregnant!" she finally says, pointing at her belly.

Then her eyes moisten with tears and she lets out a short nervous laugh.

Jonathan looks down at her body. The woman is pregnant. Very, very pregnant. He doesn't think her belly is part of the costume. It looks too real. There is even some shifting beneath her skin. But, for some reason, this strange woman painted her pregnant belly red to match the rest of her costume. When Jonathan looks back to her eyes, she bites her lip-piercing and wipes the tears out of her eyes. It is as if she has been waiting to tell him this bit of news for a very long time.

Jonathan doesn't know what to say to her. He guesses the proper thing to tell somebody would be congratulations, but he's just so bewildered by the woman that he can't get himself to say it. He wonders who the hell gets so emotional over telling a stranger they're pregnant, even if the person is a huge fan of that stranger's lego creations. But he's heard that pregnant women often have strange mood swings. He decides to leave it at that.

Before he can say anything, she lunges at him. She wraps her arms around him so tightly that he can hardly breathe and buries her face into his neck. He doesn't know what to do so he just hugs her back, resting his chin between her horns. The woman doesn't let go for several minutes, just hugging him with all of her strength and moistening his orange shirt with her tears.

He stands there awkwardly, worried about her pregnant belly squishing into his torso. Upon closer examination, he realizes that her costume was brilliantly constructed. Her red paint doesn't rub off her skin as she touches him. It's almost as if she dyed her skin this color. Her horns are firm, and securely fastened to her head somehow. And he has no idea how she gets her devil tail to move through the air like that. It must move via remote control. She finally pulls back and looks him in the eyes, wiping away her tears and smiling happily.

Not sure what else to do, he says, "So, do you want a tour of the house?"

"Yes," she says, raising her eyebrows and clapping her hands together.

Jonathan catches a glimpse of her very long black fingernails that appear to be almost razor-sharp, and wonders if inviting her into his home is such a good idea. He now wishes it was a mother with her children who had come to his door this morning.

A look of amazement brightens her face as the girl in the devil costume enters the house and steps through Jonathan's lego workshop. Not even children have ever been so happy to see his wonderful creations.

"Wow," the girl says, gazing across the walls and ceiling. "It's so colorful. I've never seen so much color."

She seems more interested in the actual room than his artwork, so Jonathan leads her into his gallery area.

"Here's all of my greatest creations," Jonathan says.

The girl steps casually through the gallery of sculptures, looking at each of the individual pieces briefly but she doesn't seem as excited to see his art as she was to see the actual house. That is, until she comes across the devil man in the wheelchair.

"Hey, you did one of Uncle Xexus," she says with a big smile.

Jonathan doesn't know who she's referring to. "I built it yesterday."

"It looks just like him," she says.

Pointing at his library of photo albums on the far wall, he says, "And this is my collection of complete works."

The girl looks at the albums and nods her head. Then she looks back at Jonathan and smiles like a bashful teenager. Jonathan pulls one of the albums out and gives it to her to look at, but she just bows at him and puts the album under her arm, as if she thinks he has just lent her a book to read some other time.

"Upstairs is the kitchen, living room and bedroom," Jonathan says.

"Oh, I wanna see," the girl says, returning the photo album to the bookshelf.

"Are you sure you want to go up the stairs in your condition?" Jonathan points at her belly. "It's a steep climb."

"Yeah, yeah," she says. "I can do it. I'm strong."

Then she flexes a bicep and snarls flirtatiously. Jonathan

notices that her canines are incredibly sharp. As they go up the stairs, Jonathan realizes that this costume the girl is wearing is more than just a costume. He thinks she must have gotten body modification surgery to look this way. Like the famous reptile man or the cat-faced woman. He's heard of people implanting devil horns in their head. She could have easily done this. Then she might have tattooed her skin red and implanted fangs. He's not sure how she did the tail. It looks like it could be silicone-based, perhaps with robotic components that control its movement. The tail looks like it moves on its own, so perhaps the movements have been programmed. Jonathan doesn't want to ask her about it. The sooner he can get her out of the house the better.

He shows her the second floor. She bends down a little as if scared that she might pierce the ceiling with her horns, and says, "Comfy," as she points at the couch and chairs in the living room. The furniture has real couch cushions, but the frames are lego. They really aren't actually very comfortable, but Jonathan has always been proud of his living room display.

"And this is the kitchen." He points to the other side of the room.

"There's no fire," she says to him, as she explores the tiny kitchenette.

"No," Jonathan says. "None of the burners actually work."

"I want to see the bedroom again," she says.

Jonathan wonders what she means by again. He assumes she must have seen some of the pictures he's posted online. When they go upstairs, the girl hobbles quickly over to the bed.

"It's broke," she says, pointing at all the green lego pieces on the floor.

Jonathan brushes them aside with his bare feet. "It fell apart last night. I haven't gotten around to fixing it up yet."

"Can you make the bed bigger?" she asks.

Jonathan shrugs. "They're legos. I can make it any size I want."

She smiles joyfully at his words.

"Great," she says.

When Jonathan leads her back downstairs to the exit, the girl doesn't leave. She just stands by the open door, staring at him.

"Now what?" she says.

"That's it," he responds. "That's the tour. It will be five dollars."

He holds his hand out. She looks into the palm of his hand as if expecting there to be some kind of present in it for her.

"Don't you have any money?" he asks.

She shakes her head.

Jonathan frowns and says, "Fine, whatever. It's on me. Now if there's nothing else, I'd like to get to work."

He points at the door, but she doesn't budge. He stands there awkwardly for a few minutes.

"Time to leave," he says, his patience wearing thin.

"Where are we going?" she asks.

"We aren't going anywhere," he says. "I'm staying. You're leaving."

Her smile slips from her face. "But I'm supposed to move in with you."

"Move in with me?" Jonathan takes a step back. The girl is really beginning to scare him.

Panic spreads across her face.

"Yeah, we have to raise the baby together," she says.

"What?" Jonathan's voice is shaking. He is just as panicked as the girl. He feels as if he's going to throw up at any second.

"Yeah," she says. "I have nowhere else to go."

"That's not my problem. Why don't you go move in with the father of your child?"

"What are you talking about?" she says, stepping closer and holding her belly. "You're the father of my child."

When she says this, Jonathan doesn't know what to do. He just pauses, then laughs. He thinks this has to be some kind of joke.

"Did my brother send you? Is he trying to fuck with me again?"

By the look on her face, he can tell she's serious. Her eyes are watering. There's no way she could just be playing a game with him. Jonathan decides she has to be some kind of lunatic.

"You're crazy," he says. "I can't be the father. I've never had sex with anyone before."

"But you had sex with me," she says. "Almost nine months ago."

"You have to be confusing me with somebody else."

"It was in this very house. I remember perfectly."

"I've never seen you before in my life," Jonathan says.

The girl looks over his shoulder, deep in thought.

"Oh yeah... " she says, a look of relief on her face. "I guess you wouldn't remember, would you?"

Jonathan wonders what kind of delusion her messed up brain is concocting to explain his lack of memory.

"I assumed the Memory Thief spell didn't work," she says. "But I guess I did that part right."

"What the hell are you talking about?"

She pauses, and then looks at Jonathan with a very serious face and speaks to him in a very serious tone.

"I'm a demon," she says. "A succubus... or at least I used to be."

The sincerity in her voice makes Jonathan want to both laugh out loud and run away screaming at the same time, but he holds back having any reaction at all.

She continues, "Last year, I came to your bedroom one night during the month you call July. I had sex with you. But I messed up and got pregnant."

Then the devil girl pats her belly at him.

Jonathan wants to just run away from this schizophrenic woman and call the police to take her off to the nuthouse, but he can't seem to get himself to do anything but stand there and listen.

"You don't remember right now," she says, "but you agreed to raise the baby with me if I ended up pregnant. I thought you knew that's what had happened when you saw me at your door."

After that, Jonathan has finally had enough.

"This is bullshit," he says, shaking his head. "Look, you need help. If you want I can bring you to a hospital where you can get the help you need. I know you think this story is true but you're not really a demon. You just had surgery to look like one."

"No, it's true!" she says. "If you let me reverse the spell you'll get your memory back."

"No, I'm done with this," Jonathan says.

"You have to," she cries, looking down at her feet with tears flooding her eyes.

Jonathan sees an opening and goes for the door, but she moves quickly. With the speed of a cat-like predator, she leaps at Jonathan and grabs him by the arms, holding him into place with tremendous strength. She pulls his face into her face and he squints as teardrops spray at his cheeks and forehead.

"Just let me do the ritual and you'll know I'm telling the truth," she cries. "We're supposed to be together. You said so."

Jonathan struggles in her grip. "Let go of me, you psycho."

Although he struggles with much of his strength, he is careful not to hurt the baby inside of her. It's not the baby's fault the mother is a freak. If he kicks and punches, he'd probably be able to get away. But he doesn't want to accidentally cause a miscarriage.

"The only way I can prove it to you is if you get your memory back," she says. "Just let me try the ritual. If you don't remember I will leave and never come back. I promise!"

"Just let me go," Jonathan says. "I won't tell the police if you just let go of me."

"But you're the father," she says. "You have to remember you're the father."

Then her eyes light up.

"Wait a minute... " she says. "I can prove that we had sex together."

Jonathan continues struggling, but she calms down quite a bit and even loosens her grip a little.

"You have my mark," she says, then looks down at his crotch. "On your penis."

Jonathan stops struggling.

"Your penis turned black inside of me," she says. "Like dipping a pen in a vial of ink, your purity was stained by darkness when you lost your virginity to a succubus. Normally the skin would only appear black when soaked in holy water, but I messed up the ritual so the blackness remained visible."

Jonathan looks at her, wondering how the heck she knew about his black penis. He wonders if she was the one who did this to him in his sleep all those months ago, just so that she could back up her crazy story. For a second, he even wonders if this woman is telling the truth. He wonders if she really is a succubus from Hell who raped him in his sleep.

"Even if you don't remember our encounter, you have to have wondered why your penis turned black overnight," she says. "Just let me perform the ritual and I'll give you back what you have forgotten."

She lets him go and he straightens himself up, rubbing out the wrinkles in his orange shirt.

"So you'll let me perform the ritual?" she asks. "Please?"

Jonathan takes a deep breath and then nods.

CHAPTER FOUR

Jonathan sits in the center of his workshop as the pregnant succubus happily draws a pentagram around him, using her fingernail. Like a blowtorch, the fingernail burns through the lego floor as if it's made of fire. When he sees this, Jonathan gets incredibly worried. He now believes the woman must really be a demon from Hell if she's able to do that, unless this is an incredibly well-planned practical joke with state of the art special effects.

When she's done, she removes her tank top and sweat shorts. Jonathan diverts his eyes, uncomfortable to be around a naked woman, even if she's not really a human woman. She places her hands against his forehead, closes her eyes, and begins a chant in a language completely foreign to Jonathan's world. Her belly rests on his crossed ankles as she recites the demonic ritual. He can feel the baby, perhaps his own baby, shifting inside of her.

Then Jonathan closes his eyes and the memories rain down into him, one drop at a time.

The night was almost like a dream. Even as it happened, Jonathan wasn't sure if it was really happening to him or not. He just went with it, as he always does when experiencing a fantasy, and didn't question whether it was all real or not.

He was drunk at the time, having come home after a night of drinking with Shoji. He had some late night toast and went right to sleep. But later that night, he awoke to a stranger in his bed.

At first, he thought it was some kind of animal. Underneath his covers, kneeling down next to him was a wiggling form. Jonathan assumed a neighborhood dog had gotten in and was snuggling up next to him for warmth. But as it leaned against him, he realized he wasn't feeling fur. He felt human skin.

Then a white light came on beneath the covers, like a

flashlight, and through the blanket Jonathan could see the silhouette of a girl. He jumped out of bed, taking the blanket with him. When he looked back, he saw a naked demon girl, frozen in a crawling position like a sneaky cat who had just been caught in the act.

The light was not from a flashlight, but hovered all on its own—a bright white ball that seemed to have a life of its own. Beneath the light, there was a book in the demon's hands. It looked ancient, and bound in something that appeared to be human flesh.

"Who are you?" Jonathan asked. "What are you doing here?"

The demon girl's green eyes glowed in the dark, staring at him hungrily. The ball of light rose into the air above her head shining down on her glistening red skin to give him a better view of her naked body. She arched her back, heaving her breasts forward. Then she opened her lips like she wanted to suck away the air between them.

"My name is Lici," she said. "I've come for you."

A long forked tongue oozed out of her mouth like a giant red slug. It slimed down her chest and coiled around one of her burgundy-red nipples. Jonathan was amazed by the size of it. It was like the tongue of a dragon, but with the color and texture like that of a human's. After she slurped her tongue back into her mouth, she crawled seductively across the bed toward him. Jonathan found himself becoming sexually aroused by her. It was strange that he found even her non-human parts to be attractive. Her horns, her tongue, her skin, even her tail seemed erotic as it curled slowly against her thighs.

As the demon girl crawled onto the lego-dragon section of the bed, it collapsed under her weight. Legos exploded into the air. She yelped, tumbled forward, and plopped head-first onto the floor.

It was an incredibly unsexy thing for her to do. Lying awkwardly on her side, her face suddenly filled with embarrassment. Jonathan could tell she was mortified with what had just happened. She wanted her victim to see her as a powerful, seductive enchantress, not a bumbling idiot.

"Are you all right?" Jonathan said.

He kneeled down next to her to help her up, but she didn't

take his hand. She wanted to turn him on, not make him feel sorry for her. She was humiliated. She sat up, hiding her breasts with her knees, and looked over at him. Then she started to cry.

"What's wrong?" Jonathan said. "Don't cry."

But by comforting her it only made it worse. She began to cry louder.

She said, "It's my first assignment as a succubus and I blew it!"

"You're a succubus?" Jonathan asked. "What's that, a demon?"

"Not just any demon. Only the sexiest, most beautiful demon women in Hell are chosen to become succubi. I was supposed to climb into bed with you and seduce you into losing your virginity to me." She pulled on one of her horns violently, as if to punish herself. "But who could possibly be seduced by a clumsy moron like me? I'm the worst succubus ever!"

Then she cried even louder, her red face glistening with tears. Jonathan didn't know what to do. He just wanted to make her feel better.

"No, you're not," he said. "I think you're a really good succubus."

She looked at him. "Really? You don't think I'm an idiot because I fell?"

"It doesn't matter that you fell," he said. "I thought you were super sexy before that."

"Sexy enough to give me your virginity?"

"Sure," Jonathan said, saying whatever she wanted to hear in order to make her stop crying.

She wiped the tears from her face and cleared her throat, then crawled over to him with an excited smile on her face.

"So you'll still sleep with me then?" she said.

"I don't know if I... " Jonathan stopped himself when he saw she was about to cry again.

Her voice was frantic when she said, "But I always wanted more than anything to be a succubus and it's my first assignment so if I return to Hell without completing my mission they won't let me be a succubus anymore and if I can't be a succubus I'll just die!"

She had to pause to breathe after speaking so quickly. Then she calmed down, and said, "Will you help me? Please?"

Jonathan looked inside of her sad demonically glowing puppy dog eyes. For some reason, she all of a sudden was the cutest thing he had ever seen. He couldn't refuse her. He just

30

wanted to make her happy.

"Okay, sure," he said, "if it's that important to you."

As he nodded his head, she said "Yay!" Then lunged at him and gave him a big hug and kisses.

She said "Thank you! Thank you! Thank you!" with each kiss she planted on his face.

The demon girl sat cross-legged on his bed with her tail pointed straight up in the air, reading her succubus training manual in order to figure out what she was supposed to do next.

"Is something wrong?" Jonathan asked her.

"Shhhhh!" she said. "There's all these complicated spells I'm supposed to do first. I don't want to mess any of them up."

After several minutes of flipping through the human-flesh-pages in the ancient succubus textbook, and several more minutes of chanting and spinning swirls of smoke through the air over the lego bed, Lici finally said, "Okay, I think that's it." She looked over at him with a shy smile. "We can start now."

She held out her hand and helped Jonathan off of the floor, then pulled him into the lego bed with her. They sat facing each other, smiling nervously.

"I've never done it before either," she said. "You're my first time."

"You're a virgin?" he asked. "How old are you?"

"I'm actually thirty-eight, but that's pretty young in demon-years. It's like nineteen for humans. I'm just barely considered an adult... though it's not very common for demons to still be virgins at my age, especially one that's training to be a succubus."

"I'm twenty-four," Jonathan said. "It's really rare for a guy my age to still be a virgin also."

The demon giggled. "That's why they assigned you to me, actually. They thought you'd be easy to seduce." She put her hand on his chest. "I can feel your heart aching for a woman's love."

"But I'm not aching for sex," Jonathan said. "I'm aching for love. There's a difference."

"Not really," she said.

"If any other succubus came into my bed I doubt they would have convinced me to sleep with them."

"Why am I different?"

Jonathan shrugged. "I don't know. You seem nice. You seem like the kind of girl I would want to date... if you were human."

"You want to go on a date with me?" She said, half-teasing him.

"Yeah, I think it would be fun."

"Well, maybe when you go to Hell we can go on a date," she said.

Jonathan laughed. He imagined what a date would be like in Hell, between a damned soul and a demon.

"I'll have to look you up if I go to Hell then," he said, but then he realized he didn't catch her name. "What's your name again?"

"My succubus name is Lice," she said, "but people call me Lici, because it's cuter."

"Lice? Why Lice?"

"All succubi are named after parasites."

"Oh... That's a pretty name." Jonathan pretended it wasn't disturbing that she was named after such a disgusting hair parasite.

She smiled at his response.

He said, "My name is Jonathan."

"Eww," Lici said, sticking out her lizard tongue and shaking her head. "I don't like it."

"You think my name is gross?"

"Yeah."

Jonathan smiled. For some reason, he thought it was pretty cute.

They stopped talking and stared at each other. The ball of light floated above them, reflecting in their eyes. Jonathan thought he could just stare at her all night long.

Then they inched closer together and let their smiles fall from their faces. Lici closed her eyes and wrapped her dark red lips around his neck. Then she coiled her tongue out of her mouth. It slithered up his chin and across his cheek. She sucked it back in just before reaching his lips and kissed him. Her lip piercing tickled his chin as her mouth folded around his.

Then she pulled off his clothes and wrapped her body around his, pressing her red breasts against his pale chest. Her skin was much warmer than a human's, as if the blood in her body was the same temperature as water in a hot shower. And just like a hot shower, her warmth was soothing against him. Her saliva entering his mouth was also hot, like steaming soup broth. It tasted somewhat spicy.

As Lici's passion heated, her kisses became more furious, her tail thrashed in the air like a bullwhip, and her hands rubbed faster against his flesh as if she wanted to touch ever inch of his body all at once. Her movements became so passionate, that she lost control of her body and accidentally poked Jonathan in the eye. Jonathan screamed and pushed back.

"Sorry!" she said. "Are you okay?"

Jonathan rubbed his eye, cringing in pain.

"Let me look at it," she said.

She pulled his hand away and examined it, her glowing green eye an inch away from his. The horn didn't actually puncture the eyeball. It just barely nicked the underside of his eyelid.

"You'll be okay," she said.

When she kissed his eye, the pain disappeared, like magic. Jonathan didn't think she had the power to heal his wound, but it did seem like her kiss had the power to control pain. It somehow made sense to him that demons might have the ability to either dull or intensify the pain of humans.

"I'll be gentle," she said, then pulled him back to her.

She laid him down on the bed and then slid her tongue up his thigh. The second it touched his penis, he became hard. Then the tongue coiled around the shaft like a boa constrictor wrapping up its prey and pulled it into her mouth. She only sucked on it for a moment, just to lubricate it and get him ready.

Then she crawled on top of him.

"Are you sure you want to do this?" she asked, his penis in her hand, just inches away from her opening. "Once you give it to me it will be mine forever."

"Yes," he said. "I want you to have it."

He meant it, too. At that moment, he felt special to be losing his virginity to a demoness. Not many guys could say they've done that.

He watched as his penis disappeared between her thighs, and then she lowered herself onto him. She was so wet that he slid right in. She took him all the way inside of her, as deep as she could, then she held him there. Her mouth was wide open, savoring this new sensation. Then she smiled in triumph. His virginity was hers.

As she held his penis inside of her like a captive prisoner, the moisture around his shaft was getting hotter. Instead of soothing warmth, it became more of a burning pain. He cringed at the feeling, but didn't try to pull out. Once Lici started to fuck him, the pain wasn't as intense. Jonathan looked at her crotch and saw his penis going in and out of her. He penis had become black, as if her demonic vagina had burnt it to a crisp.

But as she continued moving on top of him, the pain quickly turned to pleasure. The burning sensation was electrifying. He wished his entire body could be melted by her heat.

Lici arched her back, shoving her breasts into his face, moaning as she approached orgasm. He could hear legos falling from the bed and other furniture in the room as she fucked him faster and more furiously, her eyes squeezed shut. Jonathan grabbed her breasts and put them to his lips. Then she held him by the back of the neck and stabbed her nipple as far back into his mouth as she could.

When they orgasmed together, Lici's tail slapped against the bed with each pulsing of Jonathan's penis as he ejaculated. And when it was over, and she felt his cum deep inside of her, the demon girl laughed and raised her fists victoriously.

Then she looked down at Jonathan. The second her eyes met his, the smile fell from her face.

"What?" he asked, as she looked at him with grave concern.

"Your soul," she said, looking him deep in the eyes. "It's still inside of your body."

"So?" Jonathan said, examining his blackened penis.

"I thought I sucked your soul into me," she said. "I feel it inside of me now."

"What are you talking about?"

"When you had an orgasm, you were supposed to ejaculate your soul out of your body and then my vagina would have sucked it up into mine. Then I would have taken it back to Hell with me."

"What?" Jonathan pulled himself out from under her. "You never told me you were going to take my soul."

"I'm a succubus. Of course I was going to take your soul. That's the whole point."

"You said you wanted to take my virginity."

"No, if I did the spell correctly I would have sucked your soul out." She feels between her legs. "But there's something inside of me. If it's not your soul, then... "

"It's my cum."

"Your seed went inside of me?" Lici cried. "The spell was supposed to prevent you from ejaculating seed. You were supposed to ejaculate your soul!"

"It's not my fault. I didn't know."

"And I'm ovulating," she said. "I'm probably going to get pregnant now."

"Why did you do it if you were ovulating?"

"Succubi always go on missions when they're ovulating. It triggers a man's primal instinct to mate. But if I did the spell right it wouldn't have been an issue. I am a complete and utter failure... "

Jonathan wrapped his arms around her to give her comfort. Even though it seemed malicious that she planned to steal his soul, he sensed innocence in her and didn't like to see her in pain.

"What am I going to do now?" she said. "I can't return to Hell without your soul. They'll never let me be a succubus ever again. And if my father finds out I'm pregnant with a human child he's going to disown me." She cried into Jonathan's shoulder, poking his neck with her horns. "My life is over. I might as well rip my throat out and die right now."

Jonathan held her tightly.

"Don't say that," he said. "Your life isn't over."

"Of course it is."

"Maybe being a succubus wasn't what you were meant to be."

"But succubi are so pretty and respected and everybody wants to be one."

"Well, I bet you're prettier than all of those other succubi, even if you don't go around sucking men's souls out."

"You're just saying that to make me feel better," she said, rubbing her red face against his chest.

"No, I'm not."

"Yes, you are," she said, then she looked up at him. "But

thanks for doing it."

She hugged him back and kissed him on the cheek, then she put her face inches away from his face so that their eyes were very close together.

"I like being around you," she said. "If I'm really pregnant and my father disowns me can I live with you?"

Jonathan nodded. "Of course you can. If I'm the one who knocked you up then it makes sense for you to move in here. We could even raise the kid together."

"Really?" she said. "You mean it?"

"Yeah," he said. "For all we know, maybe this was destined to happen. Maybe we're supposed to be together."

Lici smiled at him. "I bet we are."

Then she kissed him on the nose.

"Okay, it's a deal," she said. "If I'm pregnant I'll come back just before the baby is ready to be born. I'll move in with you. Then we can get married and have the prettiest children ever."

Jonathan just nodded at her. He thought it was a precious fantasy, but he didn't believe it would ever come true.

She didn't want to leave right away. She wanted to stay a succubus for as long as she could, even if it was only for a few more hours. They snuggled together in his lego bed and Lici fell fast asleep. Her body was like an organic furnace against him. Her snores were like the purrs of a cat.

As Jonathan drifted off into sleep, he couldn't tell which was the dream and which was reality. He decided the one with the demon in his arms was the dream. It was a sweet, beautiful dream. But he knew that if it were actually reality, it wouldn't have been nearly as sweet.

After the entire memory returns to Jonathan, he looks at Lici and says, "I see... "

"You remember now?" she asks with a smile, putting her clothes back on.

"Yeah, I remember it all."

She gives him a big hug, but Jonathan doesn't hug her back.

"So now we can get married and raise our baby together,"

she says. "My father even approved of our coupling, as long as you promise to always make me happy."

Jonathan can't look her in the eyes. He can't believe that she actually got pregnant. He can't believe that this is actually happening.

"Did you hear me?" she says, pulling his face up to meet her eyes.

"Yeah, I heard you," he says.

"Then why aren't you super happy about this?"

"I'm sorry," he says to her. "I can't marry you."

"What?"

"I wasn't serious when I said all of that stuff to you that night. I was drunk. I didn't think any of it was even real at the time. I don't want to be a dad. I don't want anything to get in the way of my work."

"But you said... " Tears pool in her eyes.

"I'm sorry, but you'll be better off without me. I'd be a horrible father. I can't get a job to save my life. I have no money. This is no place to raise a family. You should find another man to marry, another demon or something."

"But it's your baby," she cries. "I don't want to marry another man. You're destined to be with me, just like you said."

"But I was drunk when I said that stuff. I didn't really mean any of it."

At those words, Lici's sadness becomes anger. Flames ignite in her eyes and her hair whips in the air like a wind is blowing up from the floor. Jonathan hits the ground as a surge of power flows through his room. It is like a tornado emanating from Lici's chest. Two of his lego sculptures explode and one of his walls bends out like a warped balloon.

"You have to marry me no matter what!" Lici cries.

Then she vanishes into a cloud of smoke, leaving a circle of fire on the lego carpeting where she last stood.

CHAPTER FIVE

During the next couple of days, Jonathan spends most of his time reconstructing the damage Lici caused to his house and wondering if he made the right decision rejecting her. On one hand, it is his child and he does kind of like the girl's strange innocently psychotic charm, but on the other hand he isn't fit to be a father and she's a demon from Hell who tried to suck his soul out with her unholy vagina.

It's Sunday, so Jonathan has to go to dinner at his parents' house. His parents have always thought it was important to have the whole family together for a meal at least once a week. So every Sunday, his younger brother Chuck drives across town from the university, his sister Paige and her husband and two children come down from their farm in the country, and Jonathan walks down the block from his lego house. He wishes he didn't have to go to these family dinners and he knows the rest of the family wishes he didn't come either. But his mother made up this rule and she'll be damned if she was going to break it. If she let Jonathan miss the Sunday meal, then Chuck would think it was okay if he stayed at the frat house on Sundays. Then Paige's daughter would suddenly have ballet lessons on Sundays. And Jonathan's mom will have none of that.

Sitting around the dinner table, Jonathan's family treats him as an outsider even though he's lived in that house longer than any of them. They all usually try to ignore him. His mother is always busy catching up with Paige about the kids and his dad is always busy talking about sports with Chuck. The only person left to talk to is Paige's husband, Joseph, but the only thing Joseph ever wants to talk about is Jesus.

Joseph is a born again Christian and a pastor at an evangelical church outside of town called Christ's Holy Church of Jesus. He acts like a holier than thou do-gooder, but he's really a complete scumbag. He's been cheating on his sister for years with two different mistresses he has on the side. Everybody knows about them, but nobody likes to talk about them. He has abandoned his sister and their kids numerous times to live with other women, sometimes leaving them for six months at a time without giving them a dime to support themselves, yet he still acts like he's such a great saint of a man. Jonathan can't stand the sight of him. And the rest of his family tries to avoid conversing with him even more than they do Jonathan.

"Have you been thinking about what I talked to you about last time?" Joseph asks him.

Jonathan just shakes his head and keeps eating his overcooked pork chops, even though he hates pork chops. Jonathan hates all meat, actually. He's a vegetarian every other day of the week but Sunday, when his mother cooks up one of only five meal options: steak, pork chops, ribs, pot roast, or chicken. They're a meat and potatoes kind of family. But for the most part, meat grosses Jonathan out. The only reason he's eating the pork chops right now is to pretend like he's too busy to pay attention to the asshole sitting next to him. But the asshole tries to engage him in conversation, anyway.

"It's not a lot of money," the asshole says. "But I know you can use any money you can get."

For weeks now, Joseph has been trying to convince Jonathan to work as a promotions agent for the Christian Supply store. By promotions agent, he just means somebody who passes out fliers at the mall for $48 a week under the table. Jonathan swears that Joseph's church and the Christian Supply store are in business together, because during his sermons Joseph always advertises merchandise they have in their shop. Right now, it seems like they have a big scheme going on. With Easter coming up, the store has all of these Easter specials that Joseph has been mentioning to his congregation all month. He tells them that they should all make a new family holiday tradition this year that entails every member of the household buying Jesus-related Easter gifts for each other. Not real presents, but the kind of crap they sell at Christian Supply stores, like crucifixion collector's plates and resurrection nightlights. It's all a big scam to get Christians to spend more money on crap.

"Nah, I don't think it's worth my time," Jonathan says.

When Jonathan's dad hears his words, he decides to speak up. Although his dad normally ignores his deadbeat son, he never misses a chance to explain to him how worthless he is.

"You don't think having a real job is worth your time?" his dad shouts from across the table. "You just don't want to do it because it's real work, not some stupid immature hobby."

"It only pays $48 a week," he shouts back at his dad.

"It's a start, at least," his dad says.

"If I spent that time passing out fliers for my own business I'd probably make five times that much in a week."

"Bullshit," his dad says. Then he snickers and shakes his head, mumbling to himself, "Call that a business... a damn joke is what it is."

His annoying brother Chuck sits between them with his sideways baseball cap and college bookstore clothes, laughing at the discourse. He's always entertained when their father tears into Jonathan for being a loser. But what he doesn't know is that Jonathan thinks Chuck and his dad are much bigger losers than he'll ever be. His dad leads a miserable unfulfilling life and his brother is just a self-centered douchebag.

"It's not a joke," Jonathan says. "A lot of people really care about what I'm doing."

"A lot of five-year-olds, you mean." Chuck says this hoping to get laughs out of the rest of the family. He always thinks of himself as the family's comedian, but has never caught on that the Vandervoos aren't the laughing type.

His mother enters the conversation. Jonathan knows that once his mother enters the conversation, everyone at the dinner table is going to back up whatever she has to say.

"You should take the job," his mother says. "You can't live in that house forever. They're going to make you tear it down sooner or later. Then what are you going to do?"

"I'll build another one somewhere else." Jonathan has had this conversation a million times before. He hopes they don't start lecturing him about how unsafe the structure is for children or how everyone is going to think he's a child molester.

She continues, "Some day you're going to have a family and need to provide for them. Then you're going to regret not having real job experience."

"I don't want a family," he says.

"Sometimes it doesn't matter whether you want a family or not," she says. "A lot of the time it just happens. When I got pregnant with your sister it was by accident. I wasn't planning on having a family so soon in my life, but whether I wanted to have a child or not didn't matter anymore."

"That's what happened to me and your sister, as well," Joseph says. "The good Lord blessed us with a child and we knew right then and there that we had to start a family. It was all a part of His plan for us."

His mother says, "Someday you might get a girl pregnant and then you won't have a choice. You'll have to marry her and provide for the child."

"I don't have to marry a girl just because I get her pregnant," Jonathan says. "If she decides not to get an abortion and have the child then that's her own responsibility. I don't have to do anything."

He can tell his words hit a nerve with his mother, father, sister, and brother-in-law. All of them stare at him with fuming eyes.

His mother says, "You'll see. If it happens to you someday you'll realize you won't have a choice."

"It's already happened to me," Jonathan says, "and I chose not to marry the girl."

The family immediately assumes he's just lying in order to win the argument.

"Yeah right, when have you ever had a girlfriend?" his father says.

"You've got to sleep with a girl first before you can get her pregnant." Chuck laughs. "Didn't anyone ever explain how that works?"

"I'm not a virgin," Jonathan says to his brother.

"Really, Jon," his mother says. "Don't joke around about something like that. Getting a girl pregnant is not something to be taken lightly."

"I'm not joking," Jonathan says. "I got a girl pregnant last summer."

"It's not funny," his father says, slamming his fork on the table. "Don't upset your mother like that."

"I saw her earlier this week," Jonathan says. "She's probably going to have the baby any day now."

"What's her name then?" his mother asks. "Who is this mystery girl?"

"Her name's Lici. I didn't even remember who she was until she showed up at my door the other day, asking if she could move in with me."

His parents go silent. They're wondering if their son isn't telling the truth.

"Are you serious?" the father says. "Look me in the eyes. If you're lying you better say so now."

"I'm not lying."

"Are you sure it's your child?" Paige asks. As soon as she speaks, her eight-month-old begins crying in the highchair next to her. She hushes her but the baby doesn't quiet down.

"I'm positive."

The family looks at their plates for a few minutes, not sure what to say to their son. The baby's cries become screams.

His father is the first to speak, "Well, I guess you're going to have to marry her then."

"No, I'm not," Jonathan says. "I told you that I don't want to be a father."

"It doesn't matter what you want. You're going to be a father whether you like it or not, so you're going to have to take responsibility for that girl and her child."

"There's no way I'm going to marry that girl. She's a—"

His dad cuts him off, "Goddamnit, I might have let you fuck up your own life but I'll be damned if I you let you fuck this up as well. You're moving out of that house, getting a real job and supporting that woman and her child like a responsible adult."

Paige stands up and plucks the baby out of the highchair. It screams so loudly that she has to take it into the other room, but its cries are still so loud that everyone has to raise their voices to speak over it.

"You don't understand," Jonathan says. "She's a succubus. She comes from Hell."

"I don't care what she's like," his father says. "She's still your responsibility whether you like her or not."

"But she's really a succubus."

Chuck laughs. "All women are succubuses, Jon. Didn't you know that?"

Paige's five-year-old daughter begins drawing on the table with mashed potatoes. The girl's dad sitting next to her does nothing to stop the child as mashed potatoes are smeared everywhere.

"She's pure evil. She tried to steal my soul."

Jonathan sees puke draining down his sister's shoulder as she bounces the baby.

"Listen," his father says, "you're going to raise this child and that's final."

His mother has been too flustered to speak. It's finally sinking in that her son is telling the truth.

"Listen, Jon," his mother says, in a voice that's on the verge of crying. "If you need help raising the child we'd be willing to do our part. The three of you can even move in here until you get on your feet."

The father's eyes widen. He doesn't like that idea at all.

"I'm sorry," Jonathan says. "There's no way."

His mother stands up.

"Then get out of this house right now," she shrieks at him in a tone of voice he's never heard before. She speaks with such hate, such vile and disgust, that it scares him. "If you're going to abandon your child then I'm abandoning you. I never want to see your face ever again."

Jonathan can't believe how serious she is. He thought she would be at least somewhat supportive of his decisions. He looks at his father.

"You heard her," his dad says. "Until you take responsibility for your actions you're no longer a part of this family."

Joseph finally decides to stop his five-year-old as she pushes mashed potatoes onto his lap. He grabs her hand gently, but the slightest touch causes the girl to screech and whine, dropping her weight to the floor to throw a tantrum. She throws a handful of mashed potatoes in her dad's face.

As he looks at his sister and brother-in-law, he realizes how miserable they've been ever since they had children. His sister used to be a happy, energetic woman with interests and passions, but now her life revolves completely around her children. His parents are just as bad. The years of stress wrinkled into their eyes have made them cold and bitter. He couldn't possibly become like them. He couldn't possibly give up his dreams and happiness, especially for a demon woman and her hellspawn.

Jonathan stands up. "I guess this is goodbye then."

Nobody looks him in the eyes as he tosses his napkin on the floor and leaves the dining room.

"What are you doing?" he hears his mother say to his father. "Go after him!"

"Let him go," his father says to his mother. "He's a loser and will always be a loser. What else would you expect from him?"

Jonathan pauses for second when he hears his father's words and repeats them in his head for a moment.

"I'm not a loser," he says to himself, but nobody hears him, not even his sister standing on the other side of the couch.

He looks back at Paige to see that the baby in her arms is now quiet, snuggling comfortably to her chest as she rocks it to sleep in her arms. The look across her face is one of blissful joy, smiling contently down on her precious child. Maybe her life is difficult and stressful much of the time, maybe she had to marry an unfaithful bigoted jerk who makes her miserable, and maybe she had to sacrifice everything she used to think was important, but Jonathan can tell that she doesn't regret any of it for a second.

As Jonathan walks out the door, he decides that he's not the same as his sister. He could never be happy if he sacrifices his dreams. He could never be happy getting married and having a family, especially with a demon from Hell.

CHAPTER SIX

Instead of going home, Jonathan decides he needs to get a drink. He realizes he never should have told his family about Lici. They would have never found out about her otherwise and then wouldn't have made such a fuss about it. Of course, a part of Jonathan is relieved he won't have to deal with them anymore. He hasn't had a single pleasant moment with his family since the day he dropped out of college.

"You got crazy girlfriend pregnant?" Shoji asks, excitedly.

Luckily, his friend Shoji was at the bar when Jonathan arrived. It wasn't much of a surprise, though. Shoji is there almost every night. It's good to have a friend to talk to, even if the Japanese man is already way too drunk.

"Yeah, last summer," Jonathan says. "I know you're not going to believe me, but she's not really human. She's a succubus."

"A sukubasu?"

"You know, a demon girl from Hell."

Jonathan expects Shoji will think he's crazy for saying that, but instead the large man gets excited by his words.

"I love demon girl from Hell!" Shoji says. "So cute!"

"No, I'm serious," Jonathan says. "She's actually a demon who tried to steal my soul. She actually comes from Hell."

"That's super cool, demon girl is my favorite," Shoji says, knocking over an empty can of Hamm's. "Let me show you."

Shoji leans down, struggling to reach over his massive belly to pick up his Dragon Ball Z backpack. He pulls it into his lap and removes a sketch pad.

"I draw demon girl for fun," he says.

As he flips through the sketch book, Jonathan sees hundreds of manga-style drawings of demon girls. They are all cutesy cartoonish characters with tails and tiny bat wings on their heads like horns, wearing a variety of sexy outfits. Most of them are either dressed as maids or school girls. All of them flash the kawaii peace sign with big smiles on their faces.

"These are really good," Jonathan says. "I didn't know you could draw."

"I just draw for fun and relaxation when not in sumo mode," he says. Then he flips through drawings and points to a specific image, one of a demon girl flying into a young man's window at night. She's wearing pajamas and holding a teddy bear, eying the sleeping boy as if ready to pounce on him.

"Suckubasu," Shoji says as he points to the demon girl drawing, smiling at Jonathan.

"Yeah, she's a succubus like her," Jonathan says. Then he flips through an entire series of succubi-entering-windows-at-night drawings.

Although almost all of the drawings are sexual in a cutesy kind of way, none of them really seem intended to be erotic. They seem too innocent and sweet. Jonathan can't believe the massive sumo warrior would draw such things.

"It happened just like this," Jonathan says. "The succubus came into my room one night and had sex with me. Now she's pregnant."

Shoji doesn't doubt Jonathan's story for a second.

"You're so lucky to have demon girlfriend," Shoji says. "I always dream to one day have demon girlfriend. Does she have sister?"

He looks at Jonathan eagerly for a response.

"I don't know. I didn't ask."

"Hook me up with demon girl sister, Jonusan," he says. "I would be happiest sumo in whole world!"

Then he scans through his drawings with a big smile on his face. Jonathan doesn't have the heart to tell him that he has no intention of ever seeing the demon girl ever again.

As Shoji gets too drunk to speak English or even keep his eyes open, the three frat guys from the other night appear behind Jonathan's shoulder.

"Look who's back for more," says Freckled Frat Boy. "The fat slob and the lego loser."

They laugh and high five each other.

"Your fat friend spilled our beers the other night," says a frat boy with a New Jersey accent. "You owe us a round."

"Two rounds," says Freckled Frat Boy. "For pissing me off."

Jonathan looks over at Shoji, but his sumo wrestler friend is passed out, sleeping on top of his sketch pad. When Jonathan pulls out his duct tape wallet, he discovers that he's down to his last two dollars. He holds up the crinkled bills at them, even though it's not enough to buy a single beer.

"Not enough," says New Jersey Frat Boy. "Check your friend's wallet."

Jonathan doesn't like the idea of taking money from Shoji while he's sleeping, so he tries to wake him up. When he shakes his shoulder, Shoji slips off of the bar and drops to the floor, behind the stools. The frat boys giggle as his blubbery body jiggles on impact.

"Well," says Freckled Frat Boy, "go down there and get our money."

Not knowing what else to do, Jonathan squeezes behind the stools and goes for Shoji's wallet. He decides he'll have to pay him back for this later. It'll be easier than having to stand up to these douchebags. He moves slowly, hoping the bartender will recognize what's going on and come to his rescue. But the bartender isn't even in the room. Jonathan can see him through the window out front, having a cigarette.

Shoji is lying on his back, so accessing his wallet isn't easy. Jonathan tries turning him over, but the sumo is too heavy to budge. His hands sink between rolls of fat when he tries to get a proper grip.

"Hurry up," says Freckled Frat Boy. "You think we want to watch you fondle your fat friend all day?"

Jonathan turns to the window to see if the bartender is done with his cigarette. The second he looks outside, the bartender drops to the ground. It has to be a trick of the lighting, but it appeared as if the bartender's head had just fallen off. He assumes it was just the bartender's hat that had fallen off.

When Jonathan finally gets his hand under Shoji's blubberous hip and seizes the wallet between two fingers, the bar lighting dims down. Like a sheet of black ink, a shadow creeps up the walls of the bar and across the ceiling, blocking out the lights. The outside windows go black, as if they have instantly been covered by large curtains.

The drunks in the bar giggle and make mock-ghost noises as the light completely disappears. Jonathan peeks out from the stools to see what's going on, but can't see much more than his hand in front of his face. Freckled Frat Boy turns on a mini beer bottle-shaped flashlight attached to his keychain and shines it around the room. Everyone quiets down as they sense something is terribly wrong with this situation.

Out of the darkness, shadowy figures emerge. They move quickly, too fast to see. The silence turns to screaming. Jonathan can't see exactly what's going on, but there is a lot of movement. He hears chairs and tables overturning, bar patrons shrieking in agony, and bodies hitting the floor, as well as the sounds of ripping, tearing, and grinding of what could only be human flesh.

Jonathan can only see what is illuminated by the beer bottle key chain flashlight, but the Freckled Frat Boy moves it around so much that he can't get a good look at what's going on. The frat boy tries to get a look at the figures running through the bar, but he can't find them. They are too fast for his light. For a split second, Jonathan catches a glimpse of one of them as it dashes across the bar. It's not human. It's some kind of spidery creature with a long razor tail. A wave of blood splashes into the air as the creature's razor tail cuts through a row of bar patrons. It's thin, bony, and goblin-like. There seems to be several of these fast, slender creatures. But Jonathan can tell there is something else in the room, something much, much bigger. He can hear its footsteps crushing the tile floor beneath its hooves as it moves.

Jonathan tries to shake Shoji awake, but he's in a deep sleep, gently snoring. The noise doesn't disturb him in the slightest. A spinal column flies over the bar above them, splashing Shoji with blood.

The screaming dies down. It went from dozens of screams to just one or two, then quiet. All Jonathan can hear now is the writhing groans of a few old men as the last of their blood leaks from their bodies. As far as Jonathan can tell, the only people left on their feet are the three frat boys standing above him.

They back themselves up against the bar stools and squirm around as if they're about to crap their pants.

"What the fuck is going on!" cries New Jersey Frat Boy.

"Let's bail, bro," says Freckled Frat Boy. "Bail!"

New Jersey Frat Boy only makes it a few feet before one of the creatures leaps at him like a cat. He looks like a porcupine as knife-like claws explode out of his back. Jonathan gets a good look at it as the frat boy hits the ground. It is a female demon like Lici, but this one is taller, thinner, and more muscular. She is naked except for a metal face mask, and armor on her shoulders, hands, and tail that sport several razor-sharp blades. She thrashes on top of the shrieking New Jersey Frat Boy, slashing at his chest with her claws as if she is trying to dig through him. Her breasts and stomach are covered in blood, glistening in the flashlight's reflection.

"What the fuck is that?" cries one of the frat boys.

As the other two frat boys try to run, the demon's razor tail whips in the air, cutting Freckled Frat Boy's arm off at the elbow. The severed hand hits the ground next to Jonathan's foot, still holding the beer bottle flashlight. The light faces Jonathan, so he can't see anything happening in the dark. He hears movement as the frat boys try to flee, then screams, then silence.

Jonathan shakes Shoji. He has to get out of there but he hates the idea of leaving his friend behind.

"Wake up," he whispers. "Come on, Shoji."

But the sumo wrestler is out cold. Jonathan realizes he has to leave his friend where he is and try to get out of there by himself.

He tries to retrieve the flashlight from the frat boy's severed hand, but its fingers have too tight of a grip. He grabs the entire forearm and uses it to light his way, crawling across the floor between the stools and the bar, hoping to reach a side exit. There isn't any movement in the darkness anymore, everything is still and quiet. Before he gets to the end of the bar, he comes to a dead end: a waitress with half a face lies in his way. Her brains slide out of the open skull like bloody red eggs from a bowl.

As he contemplates climbing over the woman's corpse, he hears growling coming from the shadows of the bar. He sees a dozen pairs of glowing green eyes, staring at him. They don't attack, just watching him as he climbs out from behind the stools, aiming his light at an emergency exit.

"That's him," says a voice in the dark. A surly female voice.

When Jonathan gets to his feet, something charges him. Something enormous. The ground rumbles as it moves, pulverizing chairs and tables in its path. Jonathan tries to shine the light on it, but it's too quick. Something like stone hits him in the sides. The light flies from his hand. He finds himself lifted into the air, flying across the room. His body becomes plastered to the wall, high above the floor, held in place by two hands the size of boulders.

Blind to the massive figure in front of him, Jonathan can only smell its rancid dead-cow odor and feel its steamy breath blowing against his chest. Jonathan struggles to escape, but can't even lift the smallest of the arm-sized fingers around his waist.

Flames erupt from the creature's head like hair, brightening its face. When Jonathan sees the male demon, covered in red muscles and steel piercings, he finds himself shaking so nervously that he's unable to breathe. His horns are the size of a bull's. His hoofed feet are like anvils. His face is a distorted mess of scars and cracked bone. The demon glares at him with rage, growling, exposing dagger-like teeth. Jonathan knows this is a being of pure evil. It's like he's looking at the devil himself.

In a deep, blood-curdling voice, the demon says: "Congratulations."

Then he smiles.

Jonathan is taken aback. He isn't sure he heard him correctly. He chokes out a response: "Congratulations?"

In the light of the monster's flame hair, he sees the other demons gather around them, crawling like spiders. All of them wear metal masks and bladed armor, like the female demon that killed the frat boy. They clank their metal claws together as if they're applauding.

"You're going to be a father," says the demon, in an almost pleasant manner. "I thought congratulations would be in order."

Jonathan looks away from his blood-red eyes, not sure if he should scream or thank him.

"But that is not why I'm here," he says. "I came on behalf of my sister, Lici. She says you don't want to marry her. You made her very, very sad."

"I'm sorry... " Jonathan says, wiggling in the demon's grip.

The ogre's guttural demon voice goes even deeper as he says, "However, I assume my sister misinterpreted your words. You couldn't possibly not want to marry such a lovely young woman, especially now that she carries your progeny in her womb. Or perhaps you just didn't realize the consequences of rejecting her. Lici is the daughter of Lord Mazzur, ruler of the southwestern underworld. And I, her brother Axlox, am the general of Hell's army. And her sister, Candiru, is the queen of the succubi."

The naked demon woman, the one who killed the frat boy, steps forward and removes her mask, as if to introduce herself. Although Jonathan can't see any resemblance in Axlox, he can tell this woman is Lici's sister. She is a taller, stronger, curvier version of Lici, with long flowing black hair. Although Lici has a bit of sweetness and innocence in her eyes, this woman is pure sexual evil. She looks like the kind of succubus who doesn't seduce men in their sleep, but rapes them to death.

The demon general continues, "If you had known how much we love and protect our little Lici, you would have understood that hurting her would have put us in a very foul mood. We would have had to rip your heart out of your chest and forced you to endure ten thousand years of the most intense torture Hell could provide. But I'm sure you wouldn't find that preferable to marrying my sister, am I correct?"

Jonathan nods his head slowly.

"So you do want to marry Lici?"

Jonathan gulps and says, "Yes, of course I do."

"Delightful!" The demon smiles horrifically. "That's what I had suspected."

Then he turns to the succubi, "I'm sorry, Candiru, but we don't get to kill him today."

The demon woman spits and looks away, annoyed by this news.

"Well, it appears as though we'll soon become family," says the demon as he lowers Jonathan to the ground.

When Jonathan is standing on his own feet, the demon holds out his hand to shake, "It is good to meet you, brother-in-law."

Jonathan can get his hand around only one of the demon's fingers when he shakes. The other demons crowd around him, clicking their claws as if in some kind of greeting. Only the succubus stays behind, with her back to the crowd.

"The wedding will be in three moons," says the demon, as he turns away. "You can make the arrangements with my sister."

"Three moons?" Jonathan asks. "You mean three days? That soon?"

"It would be dishonorable if my sister had her child out of wedlock," he says. "There isn't much time to waste."

All of the demons follow Axlox as he takes his leave, following the light of his flame hair, except for the succubus. She stays in the shadows with Jonathan.

The succubus turns to him and approaches. She gets so close to him that her bloody breasts are nearly poking him in the chest, her face only inches away. She glares at him and growls.

Then she says, "Make her happy or you will suffer more than anyone has ever suffered," and pushes him onto the ground, into a pool of blood.

After the demons leave, the lights in the bar come back on, revealing the carnage that has been left in their wake. Gore and human body parts are sprayed across the room. Unholy symbols and spells are painted on the walls with blood. A dozen skinless heads dangle from the ceiling by their spinal cords, organized in a circle. Limbless naked torsos are impaled on stakes in the center of the room. It's almost as if the demons had decorated the room to be some kind of psychotic work of art.

At the sight of it all, Jonathan squirms in the pool of blood, trying to get up but his hands only slide in the gore. He has no idea how the demons were able to create such a horrific arrangement in such a short amount of time. On the back wall, written in blood, are the words: "Welcome to the family."

When Jonathan gets to his feet, he runs for the door, but then stops as he hears snoring. Shoji is still under the bar, fast asleep. The demons left him unscathed. As Jonathan approaches the bar, something leaps out of a pile of corpses at him. It wraps around him and nearly knocks him to the ground.

Jonathan realizes it is Freckled Frat Boy, still alive. He

clutches his remaining half of arm, holding in the blood with a tourniquet he made out of a Nike shoelace. The kid must have survived by hiding under the bodies of his dead friends.

"What the fuck was that?" he yells at Jonathan. "Why did they let you live?"

Jonathan doesn't know how to answer the frantic kid.

"It's your fault, isn't it?" he says. "They came for you. You're one of them!"

The frat kid backs away.

"No, I'm not," Jonathan cries. "They just want me to marry one of them."

"They're coming! Hell is coming to Earth!"

The kid goes for the door. "It's the final battle between good and evil!" He points his remaining arm at Jonathan. "You're on the wrong side, bro. You better fucking watch yourself!"

When the frat boy runs out of the bar, Jonathan can hear him screaming through the streets. "Demons! The fucking demons are coming!"

Looking around the room, Jonathan realizes he has to get out of there quick before the cops show up. He wouldn't be able to explain any of this. But first he has to get Shoji up. He tries shaking him awake, but it only makes him snore louder. He wonders how the heck he's going to carry him out of there.

With the unconscious sumo wrestler strapped to a dolly that the bar used for moving beer kegs, he takes the back streets to get as far away from the bar as possible. It is slow going as he attempts to wheel the five hundred pound man home, but Shoji doesn't live too far away so it doesn't take too long. He drops the man off in his backyard, putting the sketch book and Dragon Ball Z backpack under his head as a pillow. As he stares at the sleeping sumo, he realizes how lucky the fat man is for being such an alcoholic. If he didn't pass out he would have been among the mutilated corpses back at the bar. This way he won't even know what had happened.

On the walk home, it dawns on Jonathan that all of those deaths really were all because of him, just as the crazed frat boy said. His best friend might have been killed as well, all because he didn't agree to marry the demon girl. He wonders if everything would have been fine if he just sucked up his pride and married her as he had promised all those months ago.

He decides he doesn't have a choice anymore. In three days, he will marry Lici. If he doesn't he will die, maybe everyone he knows will die. He always thought becoming a husband and father would be a living Hell, but he had no idea it was going to be so literal.

CHAPTER SEVEN

When he gets back home, Jonathan can tell Lici has paid him a visit. Like a trail of flower petals, Lici has left him a trail of heart-shaped flames going from the sidewalk outside, up the steps, and into the lego house. The door is propped open and there's music coming from upstairs. As Jonathan enters, he sees the heart flames go across his workshop and up the stairs.

"What the Hell?" Jonathan yells, as he sees the flame hearts melting his lego floor.

He stomps out the fire one heart at a time, collecting melted multi-color plastic on the bottom of his shoe. He follows the trail up the stairs, extinguishing the love flames. The music he hears is some kind of slow creepy cello song with cutesy female vocals. He doesn't understand the lyrics, but the language reminds him of Japanese. It's like the kind of music a Japanese gothic lolita would listen to. But he doesn't understand how the music is playing. He doesn't have any stereo equipment or even any electricity to play it on.

When Jonathan makes it all the way up to the third floor, he realizes the music isn't a recording. Lici is sitting on a lego chair facing the doorway, singing and playing the cello. She's curled around the instrument in an almost sexual way, her legs spread around it, her tail dancing slowly through the air like a hypnotized snake. The shape of the instrument is a little different than a normal cello. It has more twists and curves with seashell-like spirals imprinted into it. It's a deep red, darker than her skin, and looks like it's made of something other than wood. It almost looks like it's carved from the bones of some giant, monstrous creature.

Her swollen belly presses against the body of the cello as she rocks gently from side to side, singing in a soft high-pitched voice. The language she sings in isn't Japanese, but some kind of ancient demonic language. Although the music is dark and creepy, it's also strangely romantic and soothing. Jonathan finds himself entranced by the music. The red skin girl doesn't look him in the eyes as she strokes the cello passionately, sensually, but he's sure she knows he is there.

When she finishes, she looks up at Jonathan and smiles.

"Did you like it?" she asks.

Jonathan nods.

"I wrote it for you," she says. "It's about how our love will last forever and overcome all odds, no matter what."

Jonathan is kind of creeped out by that, but lets it slide. He wants to yell at her for setting all those fires in his lego house, but he decides to let that slide as well. After what just happened at the bar, he's scared to piss her off.

"Did my brother and sister come talk to you?" she asks.

"Uh... " Jonathan steps back. "Yeah."

"So were they right? You didn't mean what you said before? You really do want to marry me?"

"Uh... " Jonathan takes another step back, and nods. "Yeah, we can get married."

"Yay!" she says, tossing the cello onto the bed and running at Jonathan.

"Catch me," she says, as she jumps into the air at him.

He quickly holds out his arms and grabs her by the butt as she wraps her legs around his waist and plants kisses all over his face. Because he's not very strong, he struggles to hold her up. But since she's pregnant he tries his best not to let her fall. Unfortunately, her large belly between them makes it difficult to balance. She stays on him a little too long for comfort, kissing him and looking longingly into his eyes. Her tail wraps around his wrist like a charm bracelet and one of her fangs pokes over her bottom lip as she smiles.

"You're amazingly spry for being pregnant," Jonathan says.

She crawls off of him and says, "Not really. If I weren't pregnant I would have been able to jump over your head and across the room. But I guess I am still pretty agile compared to humans."

Then she cartwheels backward—her tail whipping him in the face—to prove her point.

"Oh, I've got presents!" she says, and runs to the corner of the room.

She brings them back and says, "For our engagement."

First, she hands him a bouquet of black roses in a skull vase. It's not a human skull, but some kind of impish monkey creature's skull. The roses are not of this world.

"Black widow flowers," she says. "They're the prettiest flowers in Hell!"

The black petals are spiky and have thin vines growing out of them like spider legs. In the center of the roses, like the red spot of a black widow, is a greenish hourglass-shaped mark. Jonathan doesn't know what else to do with them, so he decides to smell it.

As he brings his nose to the flowers, they spray a green mist at him that smells of mint and chlorine gas.

"Oh, you might not want to smell those," she tells him, taking the flowers away. "They're really poisonous. They'll probably kill you."

Jonathan instantly feels a tingling, itchy feeling in his lungs and nostrils. He coughs once, and then wheezes.

"Am I going to be okay?" he asks. "I breathed in a lot."

"Yeah, probably," she says. Then she hands him the other present.

It is a heart-shaped box that looks like a standard Valentine chocolate box, but hand-painted with cute cartoony shark-like creatures.

"Chocolates?" Jonathan asks.

"No, better!" she says.

When Jonathan opens the box, he sees squirmy movement coming from inside.

"Froggies!" she says. "They're my favorite."

Then he realizes the chocolate box is filled with small chocolate-sized frogs. All of them are alive, hopping up and down. One of them leaps out of the box, but Lici catches it in midair and stuffs it into her mouth.

She gives Jonathan a stuffed-cheek smile as she crunches up the frog in her teeth. Then swallows with a loud gulp and says, "Yummy!"

When she offers one to Jonathan, he says, "No, thanks. I've just eaten. Maybe later."

"Okay... " She eats another one and closes up the box to trap the frogs within. "But they don't live long so you got to eat them while they're fresh."

Then she looks at Jonathan, as if waiting for something. He

just stands there. She keeps waiting.

"Well?" she asks.

"What?"

"Where's your engagement presents for me?" She pouts with impatience.

"Hmm... " he looks around. He worries that she'll get mad if he doesn't come up with anything. He doesn't know what she'd be like if she gets mad.

"You didn't forget did you?" she asks.

Forget? he thinks to himself, I only just agreed to marry you an hour or two ago. How was I supposed to know?

"No, of course not... " he says. "I can make you something out of legos downstairs later... if you want."

"Make me something? Of course. I love things people make for me!"

They move the cello and sit on the bed.

"Only three moons away," she says. "We've got a lot of work to do before then. I want it to be the best wedding ever."

Jonathan nods. She looks at him and smiles, and then takes his hand in hers. Although the red skin of her palm is soft and warm, her black fingernails are hard and cold like steel against his wrist. They are also so sharp that he worries she might accidentally cut open the veins in his wrist.

"I have a request to make," she says.

"What's that?"

"Um... " She blushes and looks away from him. Then she looks back. "Can we change your name? I don't want to call you Jonathan. It's too gross."

"Why is it gross?"

"In Hell, it's another name for a penis," she says.

"Oh... " he says, slightly embarrassed. "I guess you can call me something else then."

"What do you want me to call you?"

"How about Caspian?" Jonathan asks. "I always wished my name was Caspian."

"No," she says, firmly.

"You don't like Caspian?"

"No."

"Then what about Michael?"

"Nah," she says, "Too biblical."

"Greg?"

She shakes her head in disgust and grabs the box of frogs.

"Jake? Sammy? Legbo?"

With each name he mentions, Lici pops a frog into her mouth and shakes her head. She doesn't like any of them.

"Well, why don't you pick one then?" he says.

As she opens her mouth to pop another squirming frog inside, she pauses and thinks about it.

"Hmmm... " she says, her eyes rolling around in thought.

When her eyes go back down to the tiny frog in her hand, she says, "I know! It's perfect!"

"What?"

She holds up the little frog to Jonathan and says, "Froggy!"

"You want to call me Froggy?"

"Yeah, it's the perfect name for you. I love you and I love froggies, so it makes sense."

He says, "I guess you can call me that... "

She smiles excitedly and pops the frog between her lips. When she bites down, frog juice squirts from her teeth and splashes Jonathan on the cheek. He cringes when he sees the mushed up frog guts inside her smiling mouth.

"Oops," she says, when she sees the frog juice on Jonathan's cheek.

She leans in close to him and licks the goop off of his cheek with her long lizard tongue. It sends a shiver up Jonathan's spine.

Downstairs in the workshop, the ceiling flashlights are running low on battery power so Lici uses her demon magic to brighten the room. Glowing orbs hover in the air over Jonathan's lego sculptures, as he builds her an engagement present.

She covers her eyes with her fingers, a bright smile on her face, not wanting to see her present until it's finished. Jonathan doesn't know what she would like in a lego sculpture, but she demands he make three. A man always has to give more gifts to his woman than she gives to him, she told him. So you have to make at least three. So Jonathan is stuck having to come up with three sculptures, even though coming up with a concept for just one is hard enough. It doesn't help that Lici asks, are they ready yet? every other minute. Luckily, he is fast at lego-building.

As quick as he can, Jonathan whips up a life-sized cello. He knows she plays the cello, so he figures she'd like that. Then he builds a lego goblin-like creature with a smiling face. And last is a big green lego frog.

"Okay, they're ready," he says.

When she opens her eyes, her mouth widens so big that her giant tongue flies out. "Oh wow! These are really colorful! Nothing is this colorful in Hell."

"You like them?" he asks.

"I love them," she says, running over to check out the creations. She gently picks up the frog, careful not to break it.

"How do you make it hop?" she asks.

"Hop?"

"Yeah, how do you turn it on? How do I make it move?"

"It doesn't turn on. It's made of legos. It's a sculpture."

"Oh... " she says. Then she turns to him. "Can I make it come alive?"

"What do you mean?"

"I can use my magic on it," she says. "So that it will hop."

Jonathan likes the idea of seeing the lego frog hop, if she can really use magic to make it happen. She places her hand on the frog and chants in the demon language. Then the frog pops into life. It wiggles its lego legs and blinks its lego eyes.

"It's alive?" Jonathan says with amazement. "It's really alive!"

She sets the frog down and it hops in a circle around her.

"Yay!" Lici says, clapping her hands.

Then she goes to the goblin. "I'll make this alive too."

She casts her spell and the goblin springs into life. It does a little dance for them. When Lici goes to the lego cello, she picks it up and says, "This is a cute little cello. Let's see what it sounds like."

When she uses her magic on it, the lego cello becomes a real working cello. It still looks like it's made of legos but it becomes hollow and grows strings. She picks up the bow and swipes it across the strings. The sound is off, so she tunes it by twisting the lego knobs on its head.

"Oh, it sounds sweet," she says as she plays a few notes. "I put lots of love into the magic so it would sound extra nice."

"Love?" He wonders if he heard her correctly.

"Yeah, spells feed on the caster's emotions. Since I was happy when I made them, all of these creations are nice and happy."

She plays a happy tune on her cello, the lego frog and goblin dance to the music, circling around her. Then she sings. It's like some kind of demonic nursery song.

Jonathan watches with amazement as they dance. He can't believe his creations have come to life like this. The demon girl has elevated his artwork into something bigger and more wonderful than it has ever been before. When he looks at all of his other sculptures in the gallery area, he gets an idea.

"Lici," he asks. "Do you think you can make more of them come to life?"

He points at his sculptures.

"Those are my best works of art," he says. "I would love to see them brought to life."

Lici stops playing and smiles at him. "Of course, I'll do anything for my darling Froggy!"

For the next hour, Lici and Jonathan bring more of his sculptures to life and the room fills with excitement. Lego helicopters fly through the air, lego dogs bark, lego Christmas trees sparkle and shimmer, and a crowd of lego people stand in the corner chit-chatting and drinking lego wine. It has become like some kind of mad Toy Land party.

When Lici brings to life the wheelchair-bound lego demon santa thing that Jonathan made a few days ago, the thing blinks its eyes and smiles creepily up at them. He really didn't want her to make this one come to life, but she insisted.

"Uncle Xexus!" she says to the wheelchair demon. "Welcome to the party!"

He looks up at her, and says in a scratchy old man voice, "Oh, Lici. How are you doing today?" His voice doesn't go with the movements of his lego lips very well, as though his words have been dubbed like some kind of creepy stop-motion animated film.

"I'm having fun with my fiancé, Uncle Xexus!" she says, and takes Jonathan by the arm to introduce him. "His name is Froggy. Isn't that the best name for him?"

"Oh, hello there, young man," says the wheelchair demon. "I'm so happy my little Lici has found such a respectable young gentleman. I'm sure it will be an absolutely splendid wedding."

Jonathan just nods and smiles, then gets away from the demon as quickly as possible.

"He's not the real Uncle Xexus," Lici says. "He's not really as nice as that."

Jonathan nods and goes to some of his more abstract sculptures. These are the ones he likes best of all. They are surreal spiral shapes that aren't meant to resemble anything at all. Just shapes from his mind. When Lici brings them to life, they just twist and spin a little. Jonathan assumes Lici has to know what the object is for them to come to life the way she wants them to, but she has no idea what these abstract sculptures are supposed to do. They just bob their limbs, shimmer with excitement, and twist in circles.

"I like them," she says to Jonathan. "These are my favorites."

She wraps her arm around his waist and lays her chin on his shoulder. Jonathan smiles. Nobody has every liked the abstract ones before. Nobody ever gets the point of them. She's the first person to ever look at them for longer than a few seconds. Jonathan wraps his arm around her waist and lays his cheek on top of one of her horns.

"We should use them as decorations at our wedding," she says.

"Really? You think we should?"

"Yeah," she says. "We can have a lego-themed wedding."

Jonathan almost cries at the thought. He doesn't know how to explain how happy that would make him. He begins to think Lici might just be the best fiancée in the world, despite the fact that she's a demon.

He says, "A lego-themed wedding would be so great."

She pulls away from him. "But we need more than this. Build more."

Jonathan builds more abstract sculptures out of legos. Lici

likes each one better than the last. He keeps building until he runs out of legos.

"I guess that's all of them," he says.

"But we still need more," she says. "We need to take some of the others apart."

"But they're already alive... " he says.

"That's okay," she says. "What's great about it is that the legos will already be filled with magic, so whatever you construct will already be alive the second you finish building it."

"Okay," Jonathan says, excitedly. "Which one?"

"How about Uncle Xexus?" she says.

She wheels the bearded demon over to them and says, "Sorry, Uncle Xexus, but we need more legos."

When he sees what she's about to do, panic grows in his lego eyes.

"No, don't take me apart," cries the wheelchair demon. "I'll die!"

When she starts pulling off his legos, he cries out in pain.

"No! Please don't!" he says.

His shrieks of agony make Jonathan wince. It sounds as if he's going through the most horrible pain anyone has ever experienced.

When Jonathan looks at Lici's face, he sees that she's just smiling at the legos she collects, completely disregarding the lego man's pain. He can't believe how coldly she can murder the lego man like that, without a single ounce of remorse. It scares Jonathan. He finds himself inching away from her as he realizes this girl isn't as sweet and innocent as she appears. She really is a being of pure evil from the bowels of Hell, after all.

When the party winds down and the lego creations all want to rest, Lici and Jonathan go upstairs. Lici wants to sleep next to him tonight, so Jonathan has to reconstruct the lego bed to be big enough for two. Even though he doesn't have a bigger mattress to be placed on the larger bed frame, he decides he'll just use some couch cushions as a temporary extension. The second the bed is complete, Lici brings the dragon-shaped bed frame to life. It growls and spits a cloud of fire over the bed.

They lie together in silence, staring at the orange and yellow ceiling. Something seems to be troubling Lici.

She turns to him and just watches the side of his face until he looks at her.

"You like me don't you?" she says.

Jonathan nods.

"You're not going to marry me just because my brother and sister threatened you, right?"

Jonathan shakes his head.

She sits up. "Then why did you say you didn't want to marry me the other day? I thought you liked me. I thought you wanted me to move in with you and raise our baby with me... " Her eyes water up. "When you didn't want to be with me anymore I didn't know what to do. How could you do that to me?"

Jonathan decides to choose his words very carefully.

"I was scared," he says. "I still am scared. I don't think I'll make a good dad."

"Why not?" she asks. "You're nice."

"I don't have any money."

"Who cares about money. That doesn't matter."

"Maybe it doesn't matter in Hell, but it costs a lot of money to raise a family here. I barely make enough to get by myself. I couldn't possibly be a good husband and father unless I had a job."

"Then why not get a job?"

"Nobody would ever hire me. I've tried. I'm unemployable."

"I bet you could get any job you want."

"No, I couldn't."

"What job would you want more than anything?"

"Well, if I could have any job I wanted... " He thinks about it. "I would want to work at Legoland and make sculptures."

"Okay, then let's get you a job at Legoland."

"It's not so easy," he says. "It would be impossible."

"Sure it is," she says. "Everything is possible and everything is easy, if you put your mind to it. I bet we could get you your dream job before we get married. Then you wouldn't be scared to be a father anymore."

Jonathan chuckles. "But the wedding is in three days. There's no way it would happen by then."

"Well, let's go there in the morning and try."

"Go to Legoland in the morning? Do you know how far it is? It's like a forty hour drive and I don't even have a car."

"I can teleport us there," she says.

"Teleport?"

"Yeah," she says. "Even though I was fired from being a succubus, I still have my succubus powers. We use them to teleport from Hell into boys' rooms at night."

"So we can just go to Legoland whenever we want?" he asks, a smile cracking his lips.

"Yeah. Any time you want."

"Oh wow," he says. "I've always wanted to go to Legoland ever since I was a kid. My parents would never take me."

"Tomorrow morning, first thing, we'll go there and show them your sculptures. They'll surely hire you on the spot!"

"Okay," he says. "Let's do it."

He puts his hands behind his head and stares up at the ceiling, trying to get comfortable on the couch cushions under him.

"I can't believe it. There's nothing I want more than to become a lego sculptor at Legoland... "

As Jonathan fantasizes about the idea, he notices Lici is also deep in thought. Her thoughts, however, don't seem to be so happy. He realizes that she's probably thinking about how she once was able to live her dream job as a succubus, but then blew it. Even though her dream job was to have sex with guys in order to steal their souls, he feels kind of bad for her.

"So they really fired you from being a succubus?" Jonathan asks. "After you left my room that night?"

She nods her head.

"I'm sorry... " he says.

He feels kind of guilty. He isn't sure why. If she had succeeded in her mission then his soul would have been sucked out and brought to Hell. He should be happy she was fired from her job as a succubus. But when he looks in her sad watering eyes, he realizes that there is a tiny part of him deep down inside that wishes she did suck his soul out. Just because it would have made her happy.

CHAPTER EIGHT

Jonathan is so excited about going to Legoland that he's shaking. As he puts on his best and cleanest Goodwill clothes—a sky blue suit and white shirt—Lici watches him with a smile so wide her lip piercing clicks against her demon fangs. She's not excited to go to Legoland, but she enjoys sensing Jonathan's excitement. She's happy to make him happy.

"How do I look?" he asks, once he's dressed and ready to go.

"Blue!" she says. She looks down at her own outfit. "How do I look?"

"Red!" he says, but she doesn't get the joke. She's not wearing any red.

She just wears her usual slobby pregnant clothes: the white tank top, sweat shorts, and flip flops. Jonathan isn't sure where she got those clothes. He doubts they make flip flops in Hell. Although her clothes aren't really suitable for going out, he realizes it's no big deal. People are going to be more focused on her demonic appearance than what she's wearing.

"Ready?" she asks.

Jonathan nods. She takes his hand and closes her eyes. As she chants her spell, a cloud of smoke spins around them and Jonathan can feel his flesh fading away.

They don't have any money to pay the admission fees, so they teleport into the center of the park. A lot of people are around when they appear, and most of them see it happen. But, for some reason, the adults shrug it off and continue on. The children, on the other hand, won't stop staring at them. They try to explain to their parents what just happened but the parents don't want to stop to listen to them.

Jonathan's eyes light up at the sight of the place. He's finally at Legoland, the greatest theme park in the country. All around him, he sees lego sculptures. Lego people sitting on benches. Lego pirates. Lego dinosaurs.

"Let's find somebody who works here and ask them to give you a job," Lici says.

"No," Jonathan says. "I want to look around first."

"Sure," Lici says.

As they wander the park, everyone stares at Lici. The adults think she's weird for walking around in a devil costume. The children are frightened of her, because they know it's not a costume at all. They all know exactly what she is and they think she's come to kill them. Lici doesn't seem to notice that she's out of place. She thinks it's strange that children keep crying whenever she comes near them, but other than that she is oblivious.

Jonathan grabs a discarded park map from a bench and examines it.

"The Model Shop is here," he tells Lici, pointing at a small building on the map. "That's where you can watch the Master Builders create lego sculptures for the park. That's what I want to be, a Master Builder."

"Then let's go there," Lici says.

"And we can check out Miniland on the way," he says.

They walk hand in hand through the park, looking at all of the great works of lego art as they go. In Miniland, Jonathan gets to see miniature lego replicas of American cities like Washington D.C., New York, New Orleans, Las Vegas, and San Francisco. Jonathan takes his time when looking at each display, examining every last detail.

"The craftsmanship that's gone into these sculptures is exquisite," he says. "But nothing I couldn't do. I specialized in cityscapes all through high school and college. I've done hundreds of them. They were all made-up cities, though, not based on real cities."

Lici just nods at him. She's not really interested in mini lego cities.

As Jonathan inspects the intricacies of the Jefferson Memorial building in the miniature Washington D.C. cityscape, Lici gets distracted when she sees a baby in a stroller. She goes to the stroller and smiles down on the baby as it sleeps. The mother is busy cleaning up her five-year-old son who has just spilt ice cream all over his Hot Wheels t-shirt.

When Jonathan turns to see Lici hovering over the baby stroller when the mother isn't looking, he rushes toward her.

Lici smiles down at it, caressing her index finger down the baby's cheek.

"Such a sweet baby," Lici says.

The mother hears Lici and turns around. Her mouth drops with shock when she sees the demon woman touching her child.

"He's cute," Lici says, then she rubs her belly at her. "I'm almost ready to birth my offspring. It's my first one."

The woman just stares at Lici in horror. Jonathan isn't sure whether or not she heard a single word Lici said, but he can tell she fears for her baby's life. He can tell she senses something deeply wrong with Lici. She can sense her evil.

When Lici brings her other hand to the stroller, the woman sees the long black razor-sharp claws on her fingers. Lici is sliding her hand behind the baby's back, as if to pick it up.

"Lici, don't," Jonathan says, and Lici freezes.

Then the woman runs and pushes Lici away from the stroller. "Get away from my baby!"

The infant suddenly wakes and begins to scream.

Lici has a confused look on her face as Jonathan pulls her away.

"What's wrong?" Lici says, thinking Jonathan is bothered about something else entirely.

The woman looks back at Jonathan with an angry face as she pushes her baby far away from the demon girl.

"You shouldn't touch other people's babies like that," he says.

"I wasn't going to hurt it," she says.

"Yeah, but you scared her," he says.

"I didn't mean to."

"It's okay, just don't do it again."

"Humans are so weird," she says, then laughs and kisses him on the cheek.

At the Model Shop, Jonathan sees a Master Builder at work. In a small workshop behind a glass wall, a guy with a goatee and glasses constructs a large model of Hogwarts wizard school from the Harry Potter books.

"Wow," Jonathan says. "That guy's amazing."

He watches as the man puts finishing touches on the sculpture.

"This is what I want," he tells Lici. "This is where I want to work. In this room. On that table. Building legos all day for a living. I bet they get paid pretty good, too."

"So let's talk to him," she says. "Maybe he'll get you a job."

Lici knocks on the glass wall, but the man with the goatee ignores her. When she knocks again, Jonathan can tell he's getting pretty annoyed. He's probably used to people bugging him all day when he's trying to work. He probably feels like an animal at a zoo. If Jonathan was working in there he wouldn't get annoyed. He'd wave at everyone who knocked on the glass.

"What a jerk," Lici says.

"He's an artist," Jonathan says. "You shouldn't disturb an artist when he's working."

Lici grinds her fists, but doesn't knock again.

Once the man is finished with Hogwarts and returns the leftover legos to their proper containers, he leaves the room through the side door.

"Let's see if we can catch him," Jonathan says.

They go around to the side of the building and meet the man face to face, as he locks the door to the Model Shop.

"You do great work," Jonathan says, then looks down at his name tag, "Steve."

"Thank you," says Steve, the Master Builder. He doesn't make eye contact.

"I've always wanted to be a Master Builder," Jonathan says. "Do you know if Legoland is hiring?"

The man snickers a little. "Not any time soon."

"He needs the job right now," Lici says.

Jonathan waves at her, signaling her not to speak. She doesn't understand and waves back at him.

"Forget it," says the Master Builder. "Everyone wants to be a Builder. The list of applicants is a mile long. You'd have better luck winning the lottery."

"But I've been building my entire life," Jonathan says. "I live in a house made of legos that I built myself."

The Builder shrugs him off, as if he doesn't believe him or

just isn't impressed.

"How long did it take you to make that Hogwarts in there?"

"Weeks," the Master Builder says. "I'm sure you think you're good, but it takes an incredible amount of skill to do what I do. It doesn't matter how many years you've been playing around with legos."

He tries to walk away but Jonathan gets in front of him. Lici takes that as a cue to cut him off from behind and gets behind the man.

"Weeks?" Jonathan says. "That long? I bet I could have made it in a couple of hours."

The man shakes his head and tries to get past him. Jonathan won't let him by.

Jonathan says, "Let me in the Model Shop for just two hours and I bet I could duplicate your Hogwarts."

The Master Builder looks around for help, but he's all alone with them.

"Please?" Jonathan says.

"I'm sorry, only employees are allowed in there," he says. "Now if you'll let me go, I'm late for an appointment."

"Let him build something," Lici says. "He can make stuff better than your stupid building."

"Just let me try," Jonathan says. "I'm really fast and really talented."

The man loses his patience. "If you don't leave me alone I'm going to call security." Then he barges through Jonathan.

"No, you don't," Lici says and grabs his arm.

The man yells, "Security!"

But nobody hears him.

Fire ignites in Lici's eyes. She grabs the man by the throat and lifts him into the air. He grabs at her wrists and gasps for breath, as a tornado of energy spirals around them, blowing leaves and papers across the alley.

"Now you're going to let my Froggy use your lego shop," she cries, her voice becoming unnaturally deep and ferocious, like the voice of her giant brother Axlox, "or I'm going to rip your innards out of your belly and hang you by them."

"Stop it," Jonathan says, looking around to see if anyone's watching.

He grabs Lici and tries to pry her fingers away from the guy's neck. When she lets go of him, the man drops to the ground, gagging and coughing.

"That's not how I want to do it," he says. "You can't threaten people into giving me a job."

Lici looks at him and frowns. Then she nods. When she looks down at the Master Builder, he shrieks and crawls to his feet. He runs away from her in such a panic that he trips over his own legs every few feet. When he gets to the other people in the park, he points at Lici, but he's too scared to even speak. He just points. All of the Legoland guests move away from him as if he's drunk, keeping their children far away from his reach.

"We should probably go," Jonathan says, frowning.

"But we haven't gotten you a job yet," she says.

"I can't get a job here," he says. "They'll never hire me, especially what you just did to that guy."

She grabs him by the shoulders and looks him in the eyes.

"You can't give up so easily," she says. "You just need to show them what you can do. If they won't let you build inside of the Model Shop then just build something out here where everyone can see you. I'm sure you'll impress everyone, even the other Master Builders. Maybe even the guy I just strangled half to death."

She smiles.

"Maybe... " Jonathan says.

He thinks about it. He worries about the Master Builder calling security on them for what Lici did, but he guesses she can just teleport them away at any sign of trouble. It might just work. Except...

"I don't have any legos," he says. "How am I going to showcase my talent without legos."

"I'll get some for you," she says.

She teleports away and five minutes later returns with a giant bag the size of Santa's.

"Is this enough?" she says.

When she hands him the bag, it's so heavy he drops it to the ground. He opens it to discover that it's filled with about three hundred pounds of legos, of all different colors and shapes.

"Where did you get these?" Jonathan asks.

She points through the glass wall to the Model Shop. The place looks like a disaster area. Tons of empty boxes are overturned. Cabinets left open. Shelves are completely bare. The only legos she left behind are those in the model of Hogwarts.

"We better work fast," Jonathan says, realizing a crowd of people are looking inside of the Model Shop wondering what had happened in there.

They take the bag of legos to a courtyard outside the Garden Restaurant. Then Jonathan begins to build. At first, everyone ignores him. He's just sitting on the sidewalk, messing around with legos. But then some children see how fast he is working and they come over to watch. His two hands work so fast not even a factory machine could keep up. The children watch with amazement as he constructs a large green turtle the size of a small merry-go-round. A security guard sees him and speaks into his walkie-talkie, but he doesn't approach. Not yet, anyway.

By the time the turtle is complete, Jonathan has drawn quite a large crowd, both children and adults. They don't notice Lici as she uses her magic to bring the turtle to life. It walks across the sidewalk, blinking and smiling at the children. They all think Jonathan works for the park and this is some kind of special attraction. Two children climb on top of the turtle and ride on its back, as it slowly walks across the sidewalk and chews on the leaves of a plant.

A few more security guards arrive behind the crowd, trying to figure out what's going on and whether or not Jonathan is supposed to be building there. They, too, assume he's some kind of special attraction.

Jonathan builds some more lego creations, smaller ones that he can do even quicker. He creates some bunny rabbits. When they are brought to life, they hop up and down at the crowd.

"Yay!" Lici says, hopping up and down with the rabbits.

The audience applauds, but the security guards look worried. They must have just heard from their bosses that Jonathan isn't actually an employee at the park. But now that he's in the center of a large mob they're going to have a difficult

72

time getting him to stop.

Jonathan decides to go for something really impressive. With all of these people watching, he needs to outdo himself. This is his chance to shine. He decides to go for a giant lego butterfly, building it so quickly that people can't help but become entranced by his unnatural speed. When complete, only twenty minutes later, it's the size of a kite. Lici brings it to life and the butterfly flaps its lego wings.

The second the butterfly takes flight, everyone gasps with disbelief. Then they all burst into applause. When Jonathan looks up at the audience, he realizes how massive the crowd has become. They fill the entire courtyard, mesmerized by his flying lego art. The applause doesn't stop. Even the security guards are applauding. Jonathan sees that a lot of the people watching are employees of the park, including managers and Master Builders. Even Steve, the Builder who refused to give him a chance, is there watching. He's far in the back of the crowd, watching with a look in his eyes that is a mixture of fear, anger, and jealousy. He's probably never gotten such an audience reaction for his work before.

Jonathan looks over at Lici with tears in his eyes and she smiles back at him. He stands and looks up at his lego butterfly as it flutters above them, then bows to the audience as they continue to applaud.

He doesn't know what else to do so he sits right back down and continues to build his magical sculptures until all of his legos have been used up.

After he's done, a bunch of employees come up to him. There is a manager, a couple security guards, and a few regular employees who just want to meet him.

"How in the heck did you do that?" says the manager. "Robotics? Remote control? That was amazing!"

"It's a secret," Jonathan says, taking Lici's hand.

"Who put you up to this?" he says. "Are you Builders from Florida?"

"No, I don't work here," Jonathan says. "I just did this for fun."

The manager laughs. "Well, that was just the damnedest thing I've ever seen. You should come here and do this more often."

"Actually... " Lici says. "He does need a job."

The manager does a double take when he sees Lici, as if he didn't notice her until just then.

"Is that true?" he asks Jonathan.

"Yeah," Jonathan says. "I've always dreamed of working at Legoland."

"Well, I'm not in a position to hire you," he says.

Jonathan frowns and looks down at his hand, his pale fingers woven between Lici's red fingers.

"But... " says the manager. "If I tell some of the higher ups about what you're able to do I bet they might be interested. Why don't you come back in a couple of days? How about Wednesday? Bill will be here then. He's the man to see. If you give him a demonstration I'm sure he'll be interested. He might even make you a star attraction of the park."

Jonathan smiles brightly at him.

"I can see it now," he says, raising his hands as if he's holding a banner, "Mobileland, where the legos come to life." He pats Jonathan on the shoulder. "What do you think?"

"I'd love to do that," Jonathan says.

"I'm not promising anything," the guy says. "If it were up to me I'd hire you on the spot, but this goes beyond my head. We'll talk to Bill on Wednesday. How does 11:00am sound?"

"Sounds good," Jonathan says, unable to stop smiling.

When the manager leaves, Jonathan grabs Lici by the shoulders and kisses her all over her red demonic face.

"You did it," she says.

"Only because of you," Jonathan says.

He hugs her tightly and whispers, "Thank you," in her ear, pressing his cheek against one of her horns.

She hugs him back and sighs, watching the big green lego turtle walking off in the distance, searching for other turtles to play with.

CHAPTER NINE

When they get back to the lego house, Jonathan is so excited he feels the need to celebrate.

"Let's get some Carlo Rossi, make some honey toast, and spend the whole day making lego sculptures for the wedding," he says.

"No," Lici says. "We don't have time for that now."

Lici draws a pentagram on the floor.

"Why?" he asks.

"We have an appointment," she says. "My parents want to meet you."

"Your parents are coming here?"

"No, we're going to them."

Jonathan steps away. "You couldn't possibly mean... "

"We're going to Hell," she says.

"But, I—"

"It'll be fun," she says. "I can't wait to show you around."

"Am I even able to go to Hell? I mean, don't I have to die first or something?"

"Yeah, you have to die first," she says, drawing symbols around the pentagram, preparing some kind of ritual.

"So how am I going to go to Hell without dying then?"

"I'm going to kill you," she says.

Jonathan backs into the corner.

"Don't worry," she says. "It'll only be for a minute. I'll stop your heart and take your soul to Hell. When we come back, I'll revive you."

"Is that even going to work?" Jonathan says.

"I think so," she says.

"What do you mean you think so?"

"It should be fine."

"What if you can't revive me when we get back?"

She looks up at him and shrugs. "I don't know... I guess we'll have to stay in Hell. I'm sure my parents would let us live there for a while until we get our own place."

"What! I don't want to live in Hell."

"Well, you might not have to if all goes according to plan."

"I really don't want to do this. Can't they come visit us here? I don't want to go to Hell."

"My parents are too busy to come here," she says. "They run the entire southwestern kingdom. They only want to see you for a minute. That's all they have to spare."

"Just one minute?" Jonathan asks.

"Trust me it will be fine," she says.

Jonathan realizes there's no way out of this. He breathes all of the air out of his lungs and grunts in submission.

Lici lies him down in the center of the pentagram. She puts her hand on his chest and chants a spell. Nothing happens.

"What's wrong?" Jonathan asks.

"Why didn't it work?" Lici says to herself, as she flips through pages in an old book. "Hmmm... I guess we're going to have to do this the unpleasant way."

"Unpleasant way?" Jonathan says.

Before he gets an answer, Jonathan finds the demon girl's hands around his throat, choking him. He tries to pull her claws away, begging her with his eyes, but she won't stop. She concentrates hard, the tip of her tongue sticking out the side of her mouth, as she squeezes the life out of him.

When Jonathan arrives in Hell, he finds himself naked in a dimly lit chamber resembling a dungeon. Lici is beside him, holding his hand. She is still wearing her clothes. Even though nobody is in the room with them, he covers his privates in embarrassment. Lucky the blue orbs lighting the room aren't bright enough to expose him too clearly. The room is warm and comfortable even without his clothes, like standing in a sauna.

"Come on, let's go," she says. "We don't have much time."

"But I don't have any clothes," he says.

"You don't need them," she says. "Humans rarely wear clothes in Hell."

When she pulls him across the room, Jonathan suddenly

feels unusual. His senses are a little off. He feels like he's walking in somebody else's skin.

Outside of the chamber, he finds himself in a grand hall. It's like an ancient cathedral of black and red stone. It's vast and empty, hauntingly quiet.

"Wait here," she says.

As Lici runs, her flip-flops echo through the hall. She exits through the iron doors at the end of the room, leaving him alone. He realizes that he's shaking. He can't believe he's actually in Hell—the Hell—waiting to meet the demon parents of his demon bride. The place is devoid of bright colors, but it doesn't look much different than a cathedral from Earth. The architecture is grand and overwhelming, but not as otherworldly or Hellish as he was expecting.

When Lici returns she says, "Come on, they're ready for you."

Jonathan goes to her and she grabs his hand, rushing him into the next chamber. Lici sees him covering his privates and she pushes his hands away.

"Don't hold your hands like that," she says. "It's considered offensive."

Jonathan feels uncomfortable exposing himself, but he complies.

"And don't get an erection either," she says. "That's even more offensive."

He finds himself in a throne room. Two demonic figures sit in thrones at the other end, too far away to make them out. Beside him, there is a row of demon guards. They are all female and dressed in the same manner as Lici's sister Candiru, when she attacked the bar. They wear metal masks, bladed armor on their hands, shoulders, and tails, but other than that their bodies are completely exposed.

Jonathan worries about being surrounded by so many naked women. It would be a disaster if he gets an erection in front of Lici's parents.

Stepping out from the row of guards, Axlox and Candiru appear. They greet Jonathan with half-assed bows. Candiru isn't wearing her armor or mask. Instead, she wears decorative green silk sleeves on her arms and a green glass tiara between her horns, but is otherwise naked. She doesn't make eye contact with either of them.

"So I see you've decided to do the right thing," Axlox says to Jonathan, glaring down on him. "Very wise choice. Come, let me introduce you to our lord and father."

When Jonathan reaches the king and queen, he notices they are both quite young. They look very much like Axlox and Candiru, in both age and appearance, but the king isn't quite as large as Axlox. He is as muscular as a professional body builder, but does not have the orge-sized body of his son. He wears only a crown and a blue robe.

The king speaks to Lici in the demon language.

Lici tells Jonathan, "My father doesn't speak English, so I'll have to translate. He has just welcomed you to his kingdom. You should bow."

Jonathan bows, fighting the urge to cover his genitals.

Lici's sister, Candiru, speaks in demon tongue and Lici speaks back in an angry voice.

"What?" Jonathan whispers to Lici.

"She wants you to turn around, in a circle," Lici whispers back. "So that my parents can estimate your value... as if you're a common slave."

Jonathan almost turns, but Lici grabs his hand tightly to stop him.

"Don't do it," Lici says. "She's just trying to humiliate me."

The king speaks again and asks for the human's name.

When Jonathan states his name, the room goes silent.

"His name is Jonathan?" Axlox says, then he bursts into laughter. "He was named after a jonathan!"

The ogre demon slaps his knee and laughs so loud the room begins to rumble. Candiru and the guards also snicker, but the king and queen do not find it amusing. Lici shrinks with embarrassment. She didn't want her family to know her groom has the same name as a penis.

"You should have said your name is Froggy," Lici says.

She speaks to them in demon tongue and says his new name is Froggy. The king nods in agreement.

As the laughter dies down, Jonathan notices that the queen is not speaking. She sits peacefully, petting a dragon-like cat on her lap. Although she too is naked, most of her chest is covered by dozens of golden necklaces and jewels. Her horns are also covered in silver bracelets all the way up, with the diamonds on the tips like stars on top of Christmas trees. When she notices Jonathan looking at her, she gives him a pleasant smile.

The king says something else that makes Lici blush and smile at Jonathan. She can't bring herself to translate the words, so Axlox has to translate them for her.

"Our lord and father said make my daughter happy with all of your heart," Axlox says. "She loves you very much."

Then the king and queen welcome Jonathan to the family and tell him they must move on to more pressing matters of state. Jonathan bows and is free to leave.

"That's all?" Jonathan asks Lici.

"Yeah, I told you they only had a minute to spare," she says, as they are escorted out of the throne room by her brother and sister.

"So we can go back to Earth and revive me?" he asks.

"Not yet," she says. "We still have time."

"But you have to put me back in my body and revive me," he says. "I thought I'd only be in Hell for a minute."

"Don't worry," she says. "I'm sure you'll be fine."

Jonathan wonders if he's ever going to get back home.

Axlox and Candiru decide to have a pre-wedding celebratory meal with Jonathan and Lici. Candiru doesn't want to be there. Neither does Jonathan.

They go to some kind of courtyard eatery on one of the balconies of the castle. The sky is mostly gray, but with hints of red and dark purple. Jonathan was imagining Hell was some kind of underground cavernous world, but it appears as though it has an atmosphere.

A few demons sit at tables around them, but they do not speak to Lici or Axlox. The three siblings are royalty and seem to be treated with fearful respect. As they sit at a stone table, human slaves quickly fill their black metal goblets with green fluid like wine.

When Jonathan goes to take a sip, Lici stops him.

"You probably don't want to drink that," Candiru says to him, coldly. "You're only a human. It could melt your insides."

"Stop playing with him," Axlox says. "It's fine."

Jonathan decides not to drink it anyway.

Soon they are served plates of food, all of which are living. There are frogs, rats, and centipedes, but there are also many creatures Jonathan does not recognize. There are orange crab-like bugs, fuzzy snake-sized worms, spiky clams, and mouse-sized goblin-like monkeys. The demons dig in, gorging on the living creatures. They swallow some of them whole, others they rip open and suck out their guts. They don't like to eat anything unless it's alive. Being vegetarian, Jonathan realizes it's going to be very difficult having meals with a demon.

The demon siblings don't speak in English as they eat their meal, so Jonathan just sits there quietly staring at the centipedes squirming on his plate. Lici puts a frog on top of his mound of centipedes and smiles, as if she's just given him a special treat he would enjoy better than the centipedes. The frog is much larger than the ones Lici had given him in the heart-shaped box. It's more like a bullfrog as big as his fist. Jonathan just looks at it. The frog looks back, staring at Jonathan with bulging eyes.

After a while, Jonathan feels completely ignored and decides to stand up and stretch. He steps away from the table and gets a good look at one of the human slaves. It is a young woman, naked though covered in soot. Her face is lifeless, devoid of all emotion. By the way she moves, it seems as if she's ready to collapse from exhaustion.

"Hi," Jonathan says as she passes him, but she doesn't give any response.

Jonathan goes to the edge of the balcony and looks down at the landscape.

The ground is far below. He must be half a mile off the ground. A moat of lava surrounds the castle, with rivers of fire trailing off in multiple directions. The rivers split through a village of tiny black buildings with blue lights emanating from the windows. The scenery is colorless and depressing. It looks as though life in Hell is very harsh. And lonely. Very, very lonely.

Jonathan feels an arm wrap around his waist and turns to see Lici. He looks back and notices her two siblings have already left.

"It's not what I expected," Jonathan tells her.

"Better?" Lici says.

He shrugs. "It's just different."

"Could you be happy here?" she asks.

"I don't know," he says.

"Most humans aren't happy here," she says. "But it's understandable. They are not treated very well."

"Are all the humans here slaves?" Jonathan asks, as he looks back at the emotionless servants serving food to their demon lords.

Lici sighs. "Not all of them. Some of them are free. Some of them live quite well. Once you die and come here, you'll still be my husband so you'll be almost royalty. You'll live better than any human in Hell."

"So when humans die and go to Hell, they just become servants for demons? I thought humans who go to Hell are tortured and punished. You know, eternal damnation."

"Well, that too," Lici says. "Most demons are on the sadistic side, like my sister. They enjoy torturing the damned souls.

"I always thought the whole point of Hell was to torture evil souls," Jonathan says, "To punish them for their deeds. And people who are good are rewarded with eternal paradise in heaven. "

She laughs.

"Humans always think that. None of you really understand the purpose of your lives."

Jonathan looks at her with a questioning face.

"You see," she says, "your world, Earth, is not real. It's like an artificial reality that God created. The purpose of it is to breed servants for our world, the world you're in now. It's kind of like a testing ground. God only wants the most loyal, pure, obedient servants for his kingdom, so he tests them out by giving them a short lifespan in your world. If a human proves to be worthy he gets to be a slave in God's country. But the other countries in our world, like Hell, get the leftover souls that He doesn't want."

"Wait, Hell is a country?"

"Yeah, our world, which is what you consider your afterlife, is just a world similar to your Earth, only people live a lot longer here. Heaven considers itself the leading country in our world, kind of like your United States. Hell is more like one of your third world countries. It's not at all as nice as Heaven."

"What other countries are there?"

"Well, you probably wouldn't have heard of most of them. A lot of countries in this world have abolished slavery and have no interest in Earth. Valhalla used to take human souls, to use in their gladiator games. But that was before their economy crashed. The gladiator arenas all went out of business."

"Oh... "

"It's mostly just Heaven and Hell competing for slaves now. But, you know what? Heaven doesn't get all the best souls all the time. Demons are tricky. We go to Earth and enslave human souls while they're still alive, before Heaven gets a chance to claim them. That's what succubi are for. They're like slave traders. Though if I would have stayed a succubus, my job would have only been to capture the humans. My sister, the queen of the succubi, is the one who sells them."

"So if you would have succeeded on your mission that night you would have sold me into slavery?" Jonathan asks.

She smiles at him. "Well, succubi are allowed to keep some souls they collect as their own personal slaves. I probably would have done that with you."

"Probably?"

"Well, probably not, but only because you would have been my first assignment. I think a succubi needs to collect at least six souls before keeping one for herself."

Jonathan is now even happier things didn't go as planned.

"But at least you wouldn't have been a slave in Heaven," Lici says. "Slaves in Heaven might live a little better and are never tortured, but there's no chance of freedom. In Hell, it's possible to earn your freedom. There are plenty of free humans here. But slaves in Heaven will never be free."

"Yeah, but you torture your slaves for fun."

"Well, some of the slaves actually like being tortured." She smiles. Jonathan can't tell if it's a wicked smile or a flirtatious one.

Lici looks out across the black mountains surrounding them.

She says, "The citizens of Hell all hate the citizens of Heaven. Our ancestors came from Heaven millions of years ago. This land was originally a prison colony for Heaven. We're all ancestors of criminals. I think that's why most demons are so angry and vicious all the time. Or it might be because our land isn't very hospitable. Our country has never really flourished. Demons lead a pretty difficult life."

Jonathan nods, but he's not sure why. He really hopes he can return to his body soon.

"I have one more thing to show you," Lici says to Jonathan. "Then we can go."

Lici takes him through dungeonous passageways and come to a door.

"It's through here," she says.

A male demon guard comes up behind him.

"Master Froggy," says the guard. "The queen wants to see you."

Jonathan is so weirded out by being called Master Froggy by a demonic soldier that he doesn't realize he's just been given an invitation to see the queen. He looks over at Lici.

"Privately," the guard says.

Lici nods at the guard and pushes Jonathan forward.

"Meet me out in the garden after you're done," she tells him, and kisses him on the cheek.

Then she disappears through the doorway, leaving Jonathan alone with the metal-faced warrior.

"This way," says the guard.

The demon leads him through corridors. Jonathan tries to memorize all of the turns so that he can find his way back, but the castle is like a giant maze. He isn't sure if it's possible to memorize the path. When the guard stops, he points to an open door at the end of a hallway.

"Through there," says the guard. "The queen is waiting for you."

The guard waits in the corridor as Jonathan steps slowly

into the doorway.

He sees the queen inside the room, staring out of a window, petting her dragon cat.

"Approach," says the queen.

Jonathan approaches and bows when she looks at him.

"Nevermind the formalities," says the queen. "You're not one of my subjects. You can relax."

Jonathan relaxes as much as he can while naked in the presence of a demon queen, who is also mostly nude. He looks out of the window to see a waterfall of lava pouring down a cliff just outside.

"I wanted to speak to you about Lici," she says. "I wanted to tell you how happy I am that she found you."

"Even though I'm not a demon?" Jonathan asks.

"I'm happy precisely because you're not a demon," she says. "Many members of our family are against your marriage to my daughter because of your race, but I'm not one of them. I believe you're the only husband who could possibly make her happy."

The queen senses the confusion in Jonathan's eyes.

"Come with me," she says, and leads him into the next room.

It is the bedroom of a disturbed little girl. There are dolls made of animal bones and dehydrated flesh, a bed decorated with skulls and flowers held up by a skeletal bedframe, childish drawings of cute spider creatures are burnt into the walls.

"These are Lici's quarters," she says. "They haven't changed a bit since Lici was a young child."

Jonathan steps forward and explores the room. There are rows of cellos on one side of the room, a row of crude handmade toys with disturbing facial expressions on the other.

"You see," the queen continues, "Lici has lived a rather sheltered life. She doesn't understand what a cruel, horrible place Hell is. Only the strong survive here. Only the most bloodthirsty of demons are allowed to flourish. Lici isn't meant for this world. She's too sweet, too innocent. If she were to have coupled with a demon man he would have corrupted her, made her either miserable or turned her into something dark and malicious. That's not what I want for her. I want to keep her the way she is. She's precious and special. She's like a bright, colorful flower growing in the deepest, blackest pit of Hell."

Then she stands face to face with Jonathan, and tells him, "The day I learned Lici's unborn child was actually from that of a human made me so happy and hopeful. I always dreamed something like this would happen to her, but I never thought it would come true. I wanted you to understand how important Lici is to our happiness, and how important you are to hers."

Jonathan doesn't know what to say, so he diverts his eyes and continues to examine the demon girl's bedroom. It reminds him of his own room, back when he lived with his parents. His room was always covered in toys and legos. If a stranger were to see it they would assume it was the room of a child's. His toys weren't as gruesome as these, but the principle is the same.

"I understand why you were initially resistant to marrying my daughter," says the queen. "You've not known her for very long and demons are surely very alien to your world, but I know you will fall in love with her if you give her a chance. You wouldn't believe how much she is in love with you."

When Jonathan looks up at her, the queen smiles. Then she points to the wall above Lici's bed. There is a hand-drawn calendar burnt into the bricks.

"For the past nine months, you're all that she has been talking about. She had been counting the days until your next meeting."

Jonathan sees every day in the calendar has been marked off. On the last day that is marked, the day that she came to visit Jonathan on Earth, there is a big smiley face with tiny hearts floating around it.

"Please," says the queen, "don't let the fact that she's a demon get in the way of your happiness. I can sense the innocence and longing in your soul. I know that the two of you belong together."

Jonathan just nods and looks away, not knowing how to respond to that. The demon queen places her hand on top of his head, like some kind of comforting gesture. Then she tells him the guard will escort him back to Lici.

When Jonathan is brought back to the place where he left Lici, he goes through the door and finds himself in a dark, empty room. Lici isn't anywhere to be seen. He wonders if the guard brought him to the wrong room.

A demon emerges from the shadows. It's Lici's sister, Candiru. She is in full armor again, staring at him with bloodthirsty eyes. He thinks it's an ambush.

"She's waiting through there," Candiru says, pointing at a pentagram painted on the floor on the opposite side of the room.

Jonathan moves quickly toward it.

"Remember what I said," says Candiru. "Make her happy or you'll have to deal with me."

Then she returns to the shadows.

As Jonathan steps on the pentagram, he finds himself teleported to another location. He's inside of a warm cavern, the ceiling opened up to the gray-purple sky. It's some kind of castle garden, full of black widow flowers, blood red ferns, glowing green vines, and venus flytraps the size of cats. A strong fragrance similar to heather tips and snapdragons is in the air. In contrast to the rest of Hell, it is like a small paradise. He looks around, but Lici is nowhere to be seen.

Jonathan steps to the far end of the garden to a small waterfall coming down from the rock walls. He puts his fingers through the water. It's warm and comforting, like a hot shower. He turns around and looks across the garden. He can tell it is probably Lici's favorite place in the castle. A place she retreats to, a place she feels at home. There is a gazebo in the center of the garden. He can picture Lici sitting under the gazebo on warm Hell nights, playing her cello for all the plants and flowers.

Two red hands emerge from the waterfall and wrap around Jonathan from behind. He turns to see Lici staring at him with a loving smile. She's naked in the water, her black hair wet and flat against her horns. She pulls his body into the warm spring and presses it against hers, kissing him through the waterfall. He wraps his arms around her and closes his eyes. Her long demon tongue envelops his and sucks it into her mouth. Then she curls her tail around his waist and lures him all the way through the waterfall, into the darkness beyond.

As they make love, Jonathan knows that he should be getting back to his body before it's too late, but with Lici in his arms he no longer seems to care.

CHAPTER TEN

When he awakes in his body, Jonathan feels an intense pain shooting through his arms and chest. His muscles are stiff and hard. His joints won't bend all the way. He can hardly sit up.

"I guess we shouldn't have been in Hell for that long," Lici says, with an after sex glow in her eyes. "You've been dead for a few hours. I had to use powerful magic to bring you back."

"Why can't I bend my fingers?" Jonathan says.

"Rigor mortis has set in," she says. "Don't worry. It will go away eventually."

"What?"

Lici smiles and kisses him on the forehead.

Jonathan props Lici up in his bed. She relaxes with a big, satisfied smile on her face, balancing the chocolate box full of froggies on her large round belly. To entertain her, Jonathan brings his lego television upstairs and puts it at the foot of the bed. When she brings it to life, she is able to watch an actual episode of the sitcom Two and a Half Men, but with all lego characters. As Jonathan leaves her alone, he sees a lego Charlie Sheen saying a wacky joke that causes the lego studio audience to burst into laughter.

Downstairs, Jonathan decides to build more lego sculptures to be used as wedding decorations. He takes apart all of the other lego creations, cringing at the way they cry as they are taken apart. But he ignores their howls. Making his wedding the best lego wedding ever is far more important to him.

Just before he finishes his first creations, his cell phone rings. It's a lego cell phone that his mother bought him so she could actually reach him when she wanted to. He took it apart and rebuilt it with legos. It works fine, but the lego buttons are kind of hard to dial. And it's a pain in the butt having to go to the public library in order to recharge it all the time.

When he answers, he can tell it's his mom. He always hates

getting calls from his mom, because she usually only calls to lecture him or give him a chore she wants him to do around her house for free.

"Jonathan?" she asks. Her voice is stern.

He pauses, debating on whether or not to hang up on her. He decides to hear her out first.

"Yeah?" he says.

"I'm just calling to see if you reconsidered your decision," she says. "I think you're making a horrible mistake abandoning that girl and her baby."

"I already have, mom," he says. "Don't worry about it."

His mother pauses, then her tone changes completely. "Really?"

"Yeah, when I met her family they didn't really give me a choice," he says. "But now that I'm getting to know her better I think it will be really good. She's even helping me get a job."

"Really?" It sounds as if she's about to cry on the other end. "I can't believe it. Really?" She pauses, as if to wipe tears away. "So you're going to marry her?"

"Yeah," says Jonathan. "This week, actually."

"This week? So soon?"

"Well, her family thinks we should be married before the baby comes."

"That's a fine idea," his mother says. "They sound like a respectable Christian family."

"Well, they're not exactly Christian... "

"Whatever denomination they belong to, it doesn't matter. I'd even be fine if they were a Jewish family." She laughs on the other line. "As long as you two are getting married and doing the right thing, I'm happy. I can't believe my little boy is finally growing up. So when do we get to meet her?"

Jonathan freezes. "Huh?"

"I'd like to meet your bride before the wedding, don't you think? How about tonight? Paige was planning to come to dinner. Why don't you bring your fiancée over, too?"

"I don't know about that... " Jonathan says.

"It'll just be for an hour or so," she says. "You can make time."

"You aren't going to like her," he says.

"Oh, I'm sure she's fine. What's her name, anyway?"

"Lici."

"Lici? Huh, that's an odd name. Is she French or something? You know your father hates French people."

"What? When did he start hating French people?" Then he shakes his head. "Nevermind. She's not French."

Jonathan's dad will wish she was only French.

"But she's a succubus, like I said," Jonathan says. "I really don't think you should meet her."

She changes the subject. "Have you made wedding plans yet?"

"Not yet."

"And you're planning on getting married this week? Do you even have a church picked out?"

"No," Jonathan says. "We don't know where we're going to have the wedding yet."

Certainly not in a church.

"Then you have to come to dinner tonight. We have a lot of work to do! I'll look up some caterers in the phone book. There's got to be somebody who could do it last minute. Don't worry, I've got money saved up for just such an occasion. We'll spare no expense." He can tell she's already clicking at her computer, scanning the internet yellow pages. "Oh, and tonight we can ask Joseph if he can do the ceremony. Maybe we could even have it at his church. This is going to be fun. I can't wait. You leave everything to me."

Jonathan becomes overwhelmed by a sense of doom.

"But... " he says.

"See you tonight," she says. "I can't wait to meet my new daughter-in-law!" Then she hangs up.

"But... " he says.

The phone slides out of his limp hand and sticks into the lego floor. He has no idea how he's going to explain Lici to his family. He wishes he wouldn't have told them when they were getting married.

When he tells Lici that his mom wants to meet her, she gets excited.

"I can't wait," she says.

"You don't understand," Jonathan says. "I don't think it's a good idea. At all. You don't know my family."

"I'm sure they'll be fine," she says.

"It's going to be a disaster."

"They're going to be my family, too, right? I want to meet them. It'll be great."

The more Jonathan tries to convince her, the more stubborn and dismissive she gets. She's even worse than his mom.

Someone knocks at Jonathan's door. He's surprised to have a visitor, considering the time. When he opens the door, he sees Shoji standing there with a couple of twelve packs in his hand.

"Jonusan!" he says, laughing.

Although Shoji has always known Jonathan lives in the lego house, he's never paid him a visit.

"Hi, Shoji," Jonathan asks. "What's going on?"

"The normal bar closed down for some reason, so I came here to drink," he says.

"I need to go to my parents' house soon, but you can come in for a while. I have something I want to ask you."

Shoji has to enter sideways, but still has a problem getting through the doorway.

"Ahh, so this is lego house?" he asks, nodding and smiling as he looks around. "It's good."

Shoji cracks open a beer and takes a seat, crushing the lego chair beneath his massive weight. He doesn't seem to notice anything wrong.

"So what you want to ask me?"

Jonathan sits on a couch across from him. "Remember I told you about the demon girl that I got pregnant?"

"Ahhh," Shoji says, smiling. "Yes, yes, yes. Cute crazy demon girlfriend. Yes, yes."

"Well, we're getting married this week."

"Oh! Congratulations, Jonusan!"

"And I was hoping you would be my best man."

The smile falls from his face and a serious look comes into his eyes. He gets to his feet. The lego house shakes a little as he moves. He stands before Jonathan, and then he bows.

"It would be an honor, Jonusan," he says.

Then he chugs his beer while still in the bowing position.

As he raises, Lici comes down the stairs. She's wearing a bright blue dress with green makeup, all ready to go visit Jonathan's parents.

"Lici," Jonathan says. "I'd like you to meet Shoji. He's going to be my best man."

Lici comes to him with a delicate smile on her face.

"Hello," she says to the sumo, with her red hand stretched out to greet him.

"She's real!" Shoji says. "I can't believe it. Just like in my drawings."

He smiles so widely that his eyes squint into straight lines. He shakes her hand rapidly and bows several times. Lici sits next to Jonathan, wrapping her arm around his shoulder. Shoji stands before them, so excited he can't stand still.

"You make super cute couple," Shoji says. "I'm so happy for you, Jonusan!"

Then he cracks open another can of Hamm's and takes a swig.

"I'm so jealous," he says. "Demon girl is my favorite."

They just stand there staring at each other for a while.

"So... " Shoji says. "Remember what I ask in bar, Jonusan?"

Jonathan doesn't know what he's talking about.

"If demon girlfriend has sister for me?"

Jonathan looks at Lici, but she doesn't seem to know what the sumo is talking about.

"Let's talk about that another time," Jonathan says, as he takes one of Shoji's beers. "After the wedding, maybe."

"Demon girl is my favorite," Shoji says to Lici, as he puts his head to her belly to listen to the fetus squirming within.

Jonathan is a little drunk by the time they walk over to his parents' house, but it's given him courage. He has no idea how his family is going to react to Lici. The alcohol has also loosened up his rigor mortis quite a bit, which has made it easier to move around.

When his mother answers the door, she starts with a big smile on her face, but it quickly fades when she sees Lici.

"Hi," Lici says, holding her belly with both of her hands.

They just stare at each other. Lici smiles wide, all dressed up to make a good first impression. His mother is not sure what to make of her.

"You must be... the girl Jonathan mentioned... " his mother says.

Lici lets herself in, walking past the mother into the home. Jonathan's mother leans in close to her son and says, "Is there something wrong with her? You know, mentally?"

Lici goes straight to the family photos on the mantle and begins collecting them in her arms.

Jonathan shakes his head. He whispers, "I told you you weren't going to like her."

"No, no," she says, looking back at the demon girl in her living room. "I'll give her a chance. I guess it makes sense that a girlfriend you'd have would be a little... off."

"Please don't bring up her... " Jonathan says, "you know, appearance."

The mother looks back as Lici spreads their family portraits across the floor to get a good look at them. When she sees a picture of Jonathan as a boy, she points at it and looks up at them with a smile.

"I'm sure no one will even notice," his mother says.

His entire family is gathered around the dinner table, staring at Lici. She smiles at all of them, happy to be there.

"So you're all going to be my new family," she says.

Every single one of them is holding back bringing up her appearance. They all want to know what the hell she thinks she's doing. It's Joseph, sitting next to her, who has the nerve to bring it up. Being a preacher, he's the one who takes the most offense to a woman dressed up like a demon outside of Halloween.

"Why are you dressed like that, young lady?" he asks. "I don't think that's appropriate attire for an evening meal."

Lici looks down at her blue dress. "What's wrong with it?"

"It's offensive," Joseph says.

Lici seems to be a little upset. She was really excited about wearing her blue dress. She has no idea he means her real skin and horns.

"Hey Jon," Chuck yells across the table. "When you said you knocked up a succubus, I didn't think you meant one for real." Then he laughs.

His mother interrupts, "I think dinner's about ready."

When she serves everyone their plates of pot roast and potatoes, Lici quickly loses her appetite. She moves the food around on her plate with a fork, but doesn't eat a bite.

"What's wrong, Lici?" asks Jonathan's mother. "You don't like pot roast?"

Lici politely shakes her head.

"Would you like me to get you something else? What do you like?"

"Anything that's still alive," Lici says. "Thanks."

The mother has no idea what she means by that.

"We have some leftover chicken? Or some salad?"

Jonathan butts in. "She'll be fine."

Lici frowns at the pot roast, wishing it were a live baby piglet with its legs tied together.

Jonathan looks under the table to see Paige's five-year-old playing with Lici's tail that's poking out of her dress. He tries to move her away with his foot. She climbs over it and grabs the tail again. When the little girl squeezes, Lici yelps.

"What's wrong?" asks Jonathan's mother.

Everyone looks under the table to see the young girl messing with Lici.

"Get out from under there this instant," Paige tells her daughter.

When Paige gets the girl out and sets her on her lap, the girl says, "She has a tail, mommy. She has a tail."

"Eat your vegetables," Paige says.

"It wags like a doggy's," says the girl.

Jonathan realizes his father hasn't said anything. He's just been grumbling quietly in the corner, eating his food, giving both Jonathan and Lici an icy glare. As soon as his father's eyes meet Jonathan's, the grumpy man decides to speak.

"So where did you go to school?" his father asks Lici.

Lici says, "I didn't go to school. My older brother and sister

93

taught me everything."

"You don't have a college degree? How about a GED?"

Lici shrugs at him.

"Great," says the father, under his breath, "another loser."

"Be nice," Jonathan's mother tells his father.

"So, kid," the father asks Jonathan. "How do you expect to take care of your new uneducated wife and soon to be born child?"

"I've got a job interview in the morning," Jonathan says.

"Oh yeah, where's that?"

"Legoland."

The dad groans. "Great."

Jonathan doesn't think he believes him.

"It's my dream to be a Master Builder at Legoland," Jonathan says. "I think they pay pretty well, too."

"It's not a real job," his dad says.

"It's what I want to do."

The dad groans again, shaking his head.

"Froggy makes the best lego sculptures of anyone," Lici says.

Nobody knows who the heck Froggy is. They decide to ignore her.

"So what do your parents do?" the mother asks Lici.

"They are very important people," Lici says.

"Are they politicians or something?"

"My father is the lord of the southwestern quadrant of Hell," Lici says.

When she says this, Jonathan's family all think she's positively insane. They all want to ignore the comment, but Joseph doesn't let it slide.

"Don't joke about such things, young lady," Joseph tells her. "God will punish you for pretending to be an agent of the devil."

"There's no devil anymore," Lici says. "He retired ages ago. He used to own the castle I was raised in, though. It's one of the oldest standing structures in Hell."

"Are you seriously trying to make us believe that you are a real demon from Hell?" Joseph asks. "Do you really want to do that?"

"But I am a demon," Lici says.

Chuck can't take it anymore. He bursts out laughing. His mother kicks him under the table until he quiets down.

"Can't you tell by my horns?" Lici says.

"That's enough," says his father. "Jonathan, end this foolishness, please."

Jonathan sees frustration in Lici's eyes. He realizes she's not going to be happy pretending it's just a costume. The truth has to come out. Then he'll have to convince his family to accept her for what she really is. Even though he knows they aren't going to like it one bit.

"It's true," Jonathan tells them.

His family looks at him.

"She's not wearing a costume," Jonathan says. "She's not a crazy person who thinks she's a demon. I tried to tell you this last time I was here but you wouldn't listen." He looks at Lici and takes her hand. "She's a demon. A real demon. And I'm in love with her."

Chuck laughs out loud and his father rolls his eyes.

"I know you're a Christian family," he tells them, "but you have to accept her for who she is. She's going to have your grandchild, who will be half-demon. I'm just asking you to keep an open mind."

"That's enough, Jonathan," says the mother, her tone of voice just as angry as it was when he refused to take responsibility for the girl he impregnated. "This girl is obviously delusional and you're only feeding her illness. This girl needs help and you're only making it worse."

"But, mom—" Jonathan begins.

"I don't want to hear another word of it," says his mother.

Paige's daughter bounces on her mother's lap and says, "She really is a demon, isn't she, mommy?"

Paige says, "Be quiet and eat your dinner. Your food's getting cold."

When Lici hears this, she looks at the little girl and says, "I can heat it up for you."

Lici reaches across the table to the little girl's plate and releases flames from her fingertips. The entire family jumps back. Their faces in shock.

"How in the Hell did she do that?" yells the father.

Joseph stands out of his seat and faces Lici.

"She truly is a servant of Satan," Joseph says.

"Sit down, Joseph," says Jonathan's father in an aggravated voice. "It's just some kind of special effect."

"Get her out of here this instant," the mother says to Jonathan. "She's scaring the children."

Joseph blesses a glass of water and throws it at the succubus.

When Lici is splashed with the water, she shrieks and falls back in her chair. The holy water burns her skin like acid.

"What the Hell did you do?" Jonathan yells.

The family sees her skin burning. They also see her tail whipping around from under her dress. Her horns not falling off as they slam into the wine cabinet. Her eyes glowing green as she cries in pain.

"She really is a demon," says Jonathan's mother.

"We must send her back from whence she came," says Joseph, holding out a crucifix from around his neck.

Paige takes her children out of the room. Chuck and the father stand up from their seats, as if they're ready to hurt somebody. Jonathan gets between his demon bride and the rest of the family.

"Don't hurt her," Jonathan says.

Lici gets to her feet with flames in her eyes. A tornado of power circles her, knocking pictures and dishes off of the walls.

"Jonathan," his father says, picking up a steak knife, "get away from her now."

"No," Jonathan says.

"That woman's a demon, son. She's trying to take your soul."

"No, she's not. She's not like other demons. I love her."

"She's bewitched you," Joseph says. "You can't trust an agent of Satan. She has to die."

"Yeah," Chuck says. "Kill the evil bitch."

"She's pregnant, you fucking assholes," Jonathan says.

"That child is the son of Satan," says Joseph. "It must not be allowed to live."

"He's right, son," says his dad. "Step away from her."

"Are you all a bunch of psychopaths?" Jonathan says. "She's carrying your grandson. She's going to be my wife."

"Not anymore she's not," says the father.

"We're getting married whether you like it or not," Jonathan says.

"God damn it, boy," his father says. "You're not marrying a god damned demon. I forbid it."

"Fuck you," Jonathan says.

He grabs a butcher knife from the counter and points it at them.

"If any of you touch her I swear to your slave-trading god that I'll cut your throat out."

The whole family creeps around the table toward Jonathan. He backs Lici away from them as she wipes the rest of the holy water away from her face with her dress. They are all dead serious. They all plan to attack.

Joseph comes at him first. When Jonathan swings the butcher knife at him, the pastor catches him by the wrist and bends it back. That's when Jonathan realizes he made a huge mistake. He completely forgot that his asshole brother-in-law knows how to fight. The asshole teaches kung fu lessons at his church, and has been training in martial arts almost his entire life.

When the knife is thrown from Jonathan's hand, Joseph lifts him off the ground, flips him over, and spin-kicks him while he's still in midair. He rolls over the dinner table and crashes through his sister's chair.

Then Joseph goes for Lici, but she ignites a ball of flame between them, keeping Jonathan's family back.

"Why don't you like me?" Lici asks, a tear rolling down her cheek. "I was nice. I really liked all of you."

"Don't use sweet words on us, demon," Joseph says. "We know your lies."

Her tears build up so much she can hardly speak. "All I wanted was to be a part of your family. I'm not evil. I'm just a demon."

Jonathan gets up and looks at her across the table. She is in such pain over what has happened. Neither of them knew it would end up like this. Jonathan looks at his mother. She's the only one who hasn't spoken up yet. His eyes meet with hers, and she has tears in them.

"I love her," Jonathan says to his mother.

His mother cries more. Then she picks up a chair and breaks it on top of the table. She grabs a leg of wood, raises it over her head like a stake, then she charges the demon.

"I won't let you take my baby!" his mother screams, running through the fire.

Lici catches the stake, holding it back as Jonathan's mother tries to pierce her through the chest. Jonathan's mother is standing in the middle of the flames as she tries to kill the demon, her clothes and skin burning.

Jonathan crawls on top of the table and jumps over his brother, pushing his mother away from Lici and out of the flames. His mother goes unconscious as she hits the floor. He looks down at her. The front of her body is black and smoldering. Her closed-minded intolerance nearly got her killed.

As the rest of the family rushes the demon with knives and crosses, Lici grabs Jonathan by the shoulder and teleports them away.

CHAPTER ELEVEN

Jonathan rushes Lici up to his shower and washes the remnants of holy water off of her skin. She checks to make sure none of the holy water got on her stomach or hurt the baby, but her blue dress prevented it. Jonathan was surprised holy water would actually do that to her. He assumes God gave this power to priests to defend against demons trying to take the souls of His slaves before they die.

When her body is completely washed, she jumps out of the shower at Jonathan and wraps her arms around him, getting his suit soaking wet.

"Your family hates me," she cries. "They forbid us from getting married."

"Don't worry," Jonathan says. "I don't care what they say. We're going to get married anyway."

"Really?"

"Yeah," he says. "Once I get the job at Legoland, we can move to California and never have to see them again."

"You won't miss them?"

"They've always hated me," Jonathan says. "I won't forgive them for what they did to you. I don't need them anymore."

"You only need me?"

Jonathan nods and she kisses his eyelid. Then she presses her cheek against his, squeezing his neck so hard that she nearly chokes him to death. Again.

To cheer each other up, they decide to make more lego sculptures for the wedding. Lici watches Jonathan work, licking the bright pink burns on her arms.

"I want to have a human wedding," Lici says. "I don't like demon weddings. They're too bloody."

Jonathan doesn't even want to know what happens in demon weddings.

"I'll wear a white wedding gown with a white bouquet," she says. "Candiru can be my maid of honor. I hope my father will be able to make it. Otherwise, Axlox will have to give me away. Where should we have the wedding?"

"I don't know, but we'll have to find a place soon."

"How about here?" Lici asks, looking around the workshop. "This is a huge room. We could easily fit all our guests in here."

"Yeah, I guess," Jonathan says. "It'll be easy to have a lego wedding in a lego house. I won't have to move any of the sculptures. Plus, having enough room for our guests won't be a problem. None of my family will come."

"Don't you have any other friends we can invite?"

"No, not really. Just Shoji. All my other friends stopped talking to me a long time ago."

"Well, we need people to sit on your side of the aisle." She looks around. "I know! You can build lego people to sit on your side!"

Jonathan laughs. "Okay. But I'm running out of legos... "

"We can take apart some of the furniture upstairs," Lici says. "You can put them back together after the wedding is over."

"Yeah, that should work."

Lici stands up, holding her belly. "Let me go get some."

"Thanks," Jonathan says, putting finishing touches on his latest sculpture.

When Lici returns, she's not alone. Walking down the steps behind her is someone Jonathan had completely forgot about.

"Look," Lici says, "I already found the first wedding guest for your side."

It's Priscilla. His lego girlfriend. He hasn't seen her for days. Lici must have found her in the secret chamber upstairs and used her magic. Now his pretend girlfriend is alive and standing before him.

"Hi, Jonathan," Priscilla says with red lego lips. Her voice is always how Jonathan imagined it.

"Priscilla?"

"You already know her?" Lici says, standing between them.

The lego girl stares at Jonathan, longingly.

"It's good to finally be able to speak to you," she says, and smiles.

When she approaches him to give him a hug, Jonathan backs away and nearly trips over his recently finished lego sculpture.

After an awkward hour of building lego sculptures—Lici and Priscilla sitting side by side, watching him—Lici gets tired and decides to go to sleep upstairs to bed.

"Keep him company, wedding guest," Lici says to Priscilla as she climbs the stairs.

When the demon girl is gone, Priscilla gets up and sits in a chair closer to him. She reaches out and strokes his cheek with her bumpy fingers. He brushes them away.

"What?" she says. "I'm supposed to be your girlfriend."

She gets off of the chair and kneels down, her yellow lego knees clicking into the lego floor. Jonathan doesn't look at her.

"So you're marrying her?" she asks. "Just because you knocked her up. How could you do that to me?"

"You weren't real before," he says. "You were just legos."

"I wasn't just legos before she came here," Priscilla says. "We were in love."

Her blue lego eyes blink at him.

"That wasn't real," he tells her. "I was pretending you were real. I was pretending you were my girlfriend. I was pretending we were in love."

"No, you weren't," she says. "You really loved me and you know it."

Jonathan can't believe he's having this conversation. He stands up.

"I'm going to sleep," he says.

"You know I'm right," she says. "We belong together."

"I belong with Lici," he says. "And no one else." He takes the last glowing blue orb from the air and goes upstairs. At the top of the steps, he looks down at Priscilla. She stays seated, staring up at him from the shadows, blowing him a kiss with her red lego lips.

CHAPTER TWELVE

The next morning Jonathan awakes to a commotion outside. When he looks out the window, there is a mob formed just outside the door. His brother-in-law, Joseph, is leading the group. His father and his brother, Chuck, are also there. Judging by the size of the other men outside, Jonathan guesses that most of them are Joseph's kung fu students from his church. They call themselves the Warriors of Jesus.

"What is it?" Lici asks.

"My family," he says. "They've probably come for you."

"Why don't they just leave us alone? I don't want to have to fight them."

"Stay here," Jonathan says, pulling on his yellow plaid pants. "I'm going to go talk to them. Teleport away at the first sign of trouble."

"But... "

"Don't worry about me," he says. "I'll talk some sense into them."

When Jonathan goes outside, they were just about ready to break the door down, but halt their attack as he approaches.

"What's going on?" Jonathan says.

"Where is she?" his father asks.

"Not here."

"Bullshit," says his brother.

"Look," Jonathan says. "There's nothing you can do to her. She's just going to teleport away if you try anything."

"Not this time," Joseph says. He holds up a net. "These nets have been blessed with power of the Lord Almighty. If she is tangled in it she will lose her unholy powers."

Jonathan ignores his brother-in-law. "Let's just talk about this."

"You want to talk, fine," says his father. "Your mother is in

102

the hospital because of that witch. She's got third degree burns covering a third of her body. She'll be scarred for life."

"It wasn't Lici's fault," Jonathan says. "Mom ran into the fire herself."

"Your mother was trying to protect you."

"She was trying to kill my girlfriend and our baby."

"Look, are you going to bring her out to us or do we have to go in there and get her?"

The crowd swarms around Jonathan, flexing their muscles, as if trying to threaten him. Jonathan notices that all of the men are armed with holy items from the Christian Supply store. There are a lot of crucifixes, but there's also some ridiculous items like Jesus collector's plates and coffee mugs with scripture written on them. Joseph probably conned all of them into buying their holy weapons at Christian Supply so he could make a commission.

"You're all making a huge mistake," Jonathan says. "She's a really nice person once you get to know her."

"We've had enough talk, son," says his father.

"But she's never hurt anyone," Jonathan says.

"Oh yeah?" says his brother.

Chuck brings a friend forward. It is the freckled frat boy from the bar. The boy doesn't look frightened anymore. He looks angry, thirsty for blood. His missing hand has been all stitched up and he wears it in a sling.

Chuck says, "Mike here says he saw your girlfriend the other night. She's the one responsible for the massacre that took place at the bar."

"It wasn't her," Jonathan says. "It was her family. She's not like them. She's not a killer."

"She's a demon, boy," says his dad. "We need to send her back to Hell."

Jonathan tries to block the door, but his father and brother pull him back. Joseph punches him in the stomach. The three of them pull him away from the door and the kung fu Christians race inside. They drag Jonathan kicking and screaming away from the house, into the street.

"It'll be over in a minute, son," his father says. "Then you'll be free."

When they let him go, Jonathan swings his arms at his family. He elbows his brother in the chest and pushes his father away from him. As he begins to run back to the house, Joseph clothesline-kicks him in the throat, sending him to the ground.

"Stay down," Joseph says.

His brother kicks him in the stomach and Joseph stomps on his back, as Jonathan tries to get to his feet. He hears a scream coming from the third floor of the lego house. Lici's scream. When Jonathan looks up, he sees her leaping down from the third floor, gliding toward him like a wingless bat. Flames ignite in her eyes and finger tips.

"Don't," Jonathan yells at her. "Just teleport away."

When she lands, she hits Chuck, knocking him across the street into a mailbox. On impact, blood splashes across the pavement. His ear rips off as it hits a jagged edge of metal.

"Chuck!" his father yells.

The boy screams and covers the side of his face, as blood sprays out, leaking down his cheek and neck.

Lici grabs Jonathan and pulls him to his feet. As the Christians charge, flames burst between them. The flames begin spinning around Lici and Jonathan, wrapping them in a tornado of fire. They stand safely in the eye of the storm.

The Christians back away as the tornado widens, stretching up into the sky. They try throwing their holy nets at the demon, but the nets just burn away as they hit the flames.

"Stay away from us," Lici screams at the crowd. "Let us be happy together."

The fire storm blows hot wind into the Christian's faces, burning shut their eyes. When Lici moves at them, the tornado follows her, spinning violently. The Christians retreat.

"We'll be back," says Jonathan's father, as he picks Chuck off the ground and carries the wounded teen away from the fire. "I won't let you defile my boy, you vile hell-spawn!"

As they back away, the tornado gets larger, filling the entire street. The asphalt and neighborhood lawns become scorched. The wind blows trash cans and lawn gnomes across yards.

"Don't ever come back," Lici yells.

When all of the Christians have left, Lici releases the tornado and falls into Jonathan's arms. Her energy is drained from using so much of her power. Jonathan lifts her into his arms and carries her into the house. He sits her onto the lego couch and fans her with his hands.

"Are you okay?" he asks.

"Yeah," she says. "Don't worry. I just need to rest."

Jonathan nods, caressing her red cheek.

"I can probably regenerate most of my power in an hour," she says. "We'll need it for your demonstration at Legoland today."

"Don't worry about that," Jonathan says.

"No," she says. "It's important. You need me. I'll come through for you. I promise."

Then she kisses his hand and closes her eyes, using his palm as a pillow.

Jonathan spends most of the hour lying beside Lici on the couch, allowing her to use him as a blanket and pillow. But when his muscles ache from the awkward position, he goes upstairs to get ready for his interview.

He takes a shower, worried about what will happen if his family returns. Both his mother and now his brother have been seriously wounded by these confrontations. He wonders why they have to be so violent toward Lici. Don't they know what will happen if she actually wanted to hurt them? Don't they know what will happen if her family finds out what they are trying to do to her? It will be a bloodbath.

Jonathan punches the lego wall of his shower, leaving white indentions on his knuckles.

As Jonathan walks naked into his bedroom, drying off on a blue washcloth, Priscilla comes up behind him and blocks the doorway. He covers his jonathan with his wash cloth.

"What are you doing in here?" he asks the lego woman, as she attempts to walk seductively toward him on her blocky legs.

"I'm here to show you what you truly desire," Priscilla says.

"You don't want that evil demon bitch. You want me."

When she reaches out to grab Jonathan's naked body, he steps back.

"I'm the only one who can make you happy," she says.

Jonathan continues stepping back until he trips on the shifting dragon tail. He falls back on the mattress. Priscilla climbs on top of him and locks her lego hands and knees into the lego bedframe, trapping him beneath her.

"I want you to kiss me like you always used to kiss me," she whispers to him.

She kisses his neck with her bumpy lips, rubs his penis with her hard plastic crotch.

She says, "I want to make love to you the way you always made love to me."

A spongy wet lego-shaped tongue emerges from her mouth and licks the side of his face. He turns away from her, tries to get out from under her.

When Lici enters the room, her eyes meet Jonathan's. She gasps and covers her mouth, tears leaking onto her cheeks.

"Lici," Jonathan says, struggling to get up.

Lici runs out of the room.

Jonathan pushes Priscilla off of him so hard that her hands pop off, still stuck to the bedframe. The lego girl shrieks as Jonathan pulls on his pants and runs after the demon girl, hoping to catch her in time before she goes back to hell and tells her family.

"Lici, wait," Jonathan says, running out of the house with his shirt and shoes in his hands.

Lici stops in the scorched section of the street, but doesn't turn around.

"Nothing happened," he says. "She jumped me after I got out of the shower." He holds up his hair. "Look, my hair is wet."

Lici doesn't turn around.

"Before I met you, I used to pretend she was my girlfriend," Jonathan says. "So when you brought her to life somehow she thinks we're actually a couple. She's in love with me."

Lici squeezes her fists.

"But I don't love her. I only love you."

Lici turns around with anger in her eyes.

"Really?"

Jonathan nods.

"She forced herself on you?" she asks.

Jonathan nods. "I tried to get her to stop."

"Then I want her dead," Lici says. "Kill her for me."

"Kill her?"

She grabs him and pulls him close. "Promise me you'll never love anyone else but me."

"I promise."

"Then kill her," she says. "Take her apart and throw away all the pieces."

"Fine," Jonathan says. "We can do that after we go to Legoland. We have to go now or I'll be late."

"I hate her," Lici says.

Jonathan hugs her and she buries her face in his shoulder, her horns poking him in the neck.

They don't go back inside the house. After Jonathan finishes dressing himself in the street, Lici teleports them to the center of Legoland. Again, multiple people see them appear out of thin air, but this time a mother gets a good look at it happening as they arrive only three feet away from her. The woman staggers back in shock, realizing what Lici really is. Lici glares at her with flames in her eyes, still upset over what happened with Priscilla. The woman screams, grabs her children, and runs away.

Jonathan wanders the park, searching for the manager who told him to come that day, but he can't find him. The manager never gave him a name, so Jonathan can't just ask an employee where he is. The manager told him the guy he needed to meet was Bill, but he doesn't have a last name. He asks a vendor where Bill is, but the vendor has no idea who he's talking about.

As they walk, Lici doesn't speak to Jonathan. She grips his hand so tightly that Jonathan at first thinks she wants to hurt him, as punishment. But then he realizes that she squeezes tighter only when he walks past beautiful women. It is as if she's holding him securely so none of the other women try to steal him away from her.

When they get to the Model Shop, they see Steve the Master Builder behind the glass. He's working on a Harry Potter Quidditch arena, complete with lego players flying on broomsticks. As Steve meets Lici's stare, he sees flames igniting in her eyes and falls back on his ass, knocking down his lego sculpture. He gets to his feet and runs out of the Model Shop, far away from them.

They wait around for a while until eventually the manager appears. He's with a group of men wearing polo shirts and khaki slacks. The manager shakes Jonathan's hand. A man with a gray beard steps forward.

"So this is the guy you were talking about, Colin?" Gray Beard says to the manager.

The manager, Colin, says, "You're going to be amazed by what he can do with legos." Then he introduces them. "Bill Shuler, this is Jonathan Vandervoo."

Jonathan shakes Bill's hand.

When Bill sees Lici, he gives her a dirty look.

"Is she a demon?" Bill asks. "This is a family amusement park. We don't like demons here. They're evil."

By the casual straightforward way Bill says this, Jonathan can't tell if he's joking or actually believes Lici is a demon. And if it's the latter, he wonders why he's so calm about being in the presence of a demon.

Jonathan says, "She's not evil. Calling all demons evil is like calling all Muslims terrorists. It's racist."

Bill holds up his hands, "Oh, well in that case I apologize. She can stay."

And that's the end of the conversation.

"Come on," Bill says, "we have a staging area for you to work."

When they get there, he sees a few familiar faces. A couple of employees and a security guard who watched him build the lego creatures the other day.

"So what are you going to build?" Bill asks.

"What do you want me to build?" Jonathan asks.

Bill puts one finger to his chin for a moment, and then says. "Make some dinosaurs. A stegosaurus, triceratops, and a t-rex. Oh, and a pterodactyl. I'd like to see one that flies."

"No problem," Jonathan says.

"You don't have to make them that big," Bill says.

"Give me enough legos and I'll make them life-sized," Jonathan says.

Bill smiles through his thin gray beard and pats him on the head.

Mountains of legos are dumped near Jonathan as he builds the giant lego sculptures. He puts them together quickly, faster than he's ever done before, constructing all four of them at the same time.

"He's fast," Bill says to Colin. "Fastest I've seen. Where did you find this guy?"

Colin shakes his head. "He just showed up at the park one day and started building. I have no idea where he came from."

"Hmmm... " Bill says.

A crowd forms as the dinosaurs reach human height. Just watching him construct the creatures is entertainment enough for people. They don't even realize that he will soon bring them to life. He can't wait to see their smiling faces as a row of children ride on the stegosaurus's back.

Lici sits behind Jonathan, still angry about Priscilla. She grinds her fists, imagining all the torturous ways she can take the woman apart. On one hand, she thinks it would be fun to hit her with a sledgehammer so hard that all of the pieces will explode across the room. That will be very satisfying. But on the other hand, it will be too quick of a death. She wants the lego woman to suffer. She wants to pull her apart, put her back together, then pull her apart again, until her screams are like music in her hears. Lici smiles wickedly at the fantasy, wagging her tail with the anticipation of bloodlust.

Jonathan has to use a lift to get up on the dinosaurs's backs to do their upper halves. Bill gives him a thumbs-up from below, as Jonathan adds the finishing touches. When they're all done and Jonathan gets down to the floor of the stage, he notices the massive crowd that has formed.

"This is going to be amazing," Jonathan says to Lici. "I can't wait to see their faces after they come to life."

Lici nods and smiles at Jonathan, but she's not thinking about the faces of the audience. She's thinking about Priscilla's face once she gets a chance to torture her to death.

The audience applauds Jonathan as he steps in front of his creations.

"Okay, make them move," Bill says.

Getting a huge adrenalin rush from the applause, Jonathan decides to address the audience.

"Prepare yourself for the magic of my lego creations," Jonathan says. "For the first time ever, you will see legos come to life."

As the audience cheers, Jonathan goes to Lici.

"Okay, your turn," he says.

Lici nods and approaches the dinosaurs. Hidden behind their massive forms, the audience doesn't see the demon girl work her magic. She brings them to life all at the same time. The sculptures shiver and pulse as they become animated. Jonathan looks up at the sculptures, breathing in his accomplishment. He realizes these are perhaps the greatest he has ever constructed.

The pterodactyl flaps its wings and takes flight. The audience gasps at its power as it soars above them.

"My, my," Bill says, nodding his head. "Now that's something."

"I told you," Colin says. "The kid is amazing."

"How's he do it?" Bill says.

But before Colin can answer, the pterodactyl swoops down and snatches him out of his shoes. The manager screams as the lego bird carries him high into the air.

Jonathan looks at the other dinosaurs and realizes something is wrong. They are growling at the crowd. Their eyes are filled with rage. When he sees the same look of rage in Lici's eyes, he realizes what's happened. Her desire to kill Priscilla has mixed with the magic, turning the lego dinosaurs into bloodthirsty monsters.

The audience cries as the pterodactyl drops Colin from its claws. The manager falls out of the sky. An explosion of blood and meat sprays across the crowd as his body hits the stage. Then the other dinosaurs attack.

Jonathan jumps out of the way as the lego triceratops charges the crowd. It tramples three families, and impales a security guard through the midsection. The audience screams and runs in a panic. Mothers try to protect their children as the stegosaurus thrashes through the audience like a mad bull. It hits a cotton candy vendor with its spiked tail, sending her flying over the river that divides the park.

The lego tyrannosaur rips a little boy from his mother's arms and bites him in half. Not with lego teeth, but real jagged t-rex teeth that have grown out of the legos. The mother shrieks in shock as the lower half of her son lands by her feet. But then she's silenced as the tyrannosaur stomps down on her, crushing her skull into the asphalt.

Bill runs at Jonathan and Lici.

"She did this," Bill yells at Jonathan, pointing at his girlfriend. "I told you, all demons are evil!"

Lici shakes her head and cries, "I didn't know it would happen!"

"You horrible, monstrous bitch," Bill yells. "There's children out there!"

As Bill charges Jonathan, the lego triceratops stampedes across the stage. It hits Bill like a semi truck, ripping him into pieces on impact. His head flies across the stage and lands in a pile of unused lego blocks.

When Jonathan looks at the carnage, he doesn't know what to do. He just stands there and watches as the dinosaurs he created trample women and children, ripping them apart with lego claws, swallowing their flesh into lego bellies. The park is littered with corpses. Blood and entrails spread across the miniature lego cities of New York and San Francisco.

He watches as the pterodactyl flies off into the distance, carrying a six year old girl in its lego claws. The triceratops chases a crowd of screaming people through the Legoland admission gate. The stegosaur tramples Steve, the Master Builder, outside the Model Shop. Red legos fly off of the tyrannosaur as it battles a security guard who defends himself with a broken sign pole.

Jonathan looks at Lici with bloodshot eyes.

"He was right," Jonathan says. "My family was right. You are evil."

"No, I'm not," Lici cries.

"You're responsible for this," he says. "You're responsible for all of these deaths. There were mothers with their babies, little kids, whole families that are dead because of you."

"It wasn't my fault," Lici says, tears drenching her red demon skin.

"How could I love someone like you?" Jonathan says.

Before Lici can respond, the tyrannosaur charges Jonathan. It has the sign pole stuck in its head and half of the security guard's corpse dangling out of its mouth. Jonathan doesn't see it coming.

Lici runs at Jonathan and pulls him out of the way. The t-rex scatters legos across the stage as it turns around, roaring at its creator. Lici prepares her magic to teleport them to safety, but Jonathan tries to get away from her. She holds him in place with one hand and casts the spell with the other. They disappear just as the dinosaur's jaws open around them.

"Get away from me," Jonathan yells as they appear on the street outside of his house.

She steps back.

"You're a horrible demon," he says. "I don't want to see you ever again."

"But... " Lici says. "We're getting married."

"You're pure evil," he says. "I don't care what your family does to me. I will never marry you."

"Don't," Lici says, softly.

"Go back to Hell," he says.

"Don't," she says, trying to speak through the tears. "Don't break my heart."

"I don't care about your heart," he says. "You killed all of those people!"

"If you break my heart my brother and sister will sense it," she says. "They'll come to kill you."

"Let them," he says. "I don't care anymore."

"But I don't want you to die," she says. "I love you."

"Well I don't love you," he says.

"You said you loved me," she says. "You promised you would only love me and nobody else."

"I didn't know what I was talking about. How could I love you? Look at you. You're from Hell. You make me sick."

"Froggy... " she says.

"Don't call me that. It's not even my name."

"Froggy... " she continues. "My heart just broke."

"Whatever." Jonathan waves her words away and stomps up the steps to his house.

When he's in the doorway, he sees her standing there in the street, crying so hard she can hardly open her eyes or keep her mouth closed. As he slams the door behind him, he hears her fall to her knees, calling for her Froggy to come back to her.

CHAPTER THIRTEEN

Jonathan realizes he's covered in blood, probably Bill's. He tries to shake the images out of his head. It wasn't just Lici's fault that the lego dinosaurs came to life and killed all those people. It was also Jonathan's. He should have known Lici was in a foul mood. He should have known she wasn't in the right mental shape to bring things to life. If he didn't push her into going, if he wasn't in such a rush to impress the Legoland employers, none of it would have happened.

He buries his face in his hands. When he removes them, Priscilla is standing in front of him. Her hands are still missing. She blinks at him and smiles her lego lips as wide as she can.

"I heard your conversation outside," she says. "You broke up with that horrible demon woman."

She comes closer and wraps her handless arms around him.

"It's for the best," she says. "You don't belong with her. You belong with me. With her out of the way, we can get married and live in this house together for the rest of our lives."

She kisses him on the cheek.

Jonathan turns away. He looks at all of the lego sculptures in his gallery, all of the sculptures that were designed for their wedding. He sees the lego cello he made for Lici propped up against the wall. He sees the poisonous black widow flowers in a happy-faced lego vase on top of his work bench.

When he feels Priscilla's body against him, he feels just cold hard plastic. He doesn't see any real emotion in her eyes. He just sees her as a pile of lego pieces in human-form

"I made a mistake," he tells Priscilla. "We don't belong together. I belong with her."

"No, you don't," Priscilla cries. "Outside, you said she was an evil demon. You said she killed people."

"It wasn't her fault," Jonathan says. "I'm the one who made her bring the lego dinosaurs to life. It wouldn't have happened if I didn't make her so upset."

Jonathan pushes her away from him.

"But I love you," Priscilla says.

"But I love her," Jonathan says, as he backs away. "And I have to get her back."

He turns and runs for the doorway. As he steps out into the street, he sees his father, Joseph, and three Christian warriors dragging Lici into the back of their pickup truck.

"Stop," Jonathan yells, running down the street after them. "Get away from her!"

A blessed net is wrapped around her, containing her powers. She cries out to Jonathan, "Froggy!"

"Dad," Jonathan yells. "Don't you fucking touch her!"

His dad looks back at Jonathan. Pauses for a moment and shakes his head. Then he gets into the driver's seat of the truck.

By the time he gets to them, the truck speeds off down the road. Lici pokes her fingers out of the net, reaching out for Jonathan, as they drive away.

"Lici!" he cries, but she's too far away to hear.

Jonathan watches the truck as it drives down the road, trying to figure out where they're heading. When they take a right two blocks down, he knows they are going to the interstate. That means there's only one place they could possibly be headed.

They're going to the place where his brother-in-law works: Christ's Holy Church of Jesus.

Jonathan runs into the house. He has to get a vehicle somehow, but he doesn't own a car or even a bike. When he sees the lego sculptures bouncing on the ground, he knows that he can reshape them into some kind of vehicle. The legos already have the magic in them, so whatever vehicle he creates will automatically work.

When he goes to the lego sculptures, he hesitates taking them apart. They are supposed to be for their wedding. He has to find something else to take apart.

Priscilla comes into his workshop and says, "You've come back to me."

As he sees her, he realizes what he has to do.

"I'm sorry, Priscilla," he tells her, as he starts removing the legos from her body. "But I'm going to need these."

Her mouth opens to cry out his name, but before any sound comes out Jonathan has already removed the legos from most of her head.

Jonathan constructs a motorcycle out of Priscilla's legos. When he turns it on, the lego engine roars. He revs the gas. Although he has no driver's license and has never ridden a motorcycle before, he's got to get to Lici as soon as possible. He doesn't know how long his family is going to keep her alive.

"I'm coming, Lici," he says.

When he gets on the lego motorcycle, he hears movement in his house, coming from up the stairs. There's a growling, screeching sound. Then he sees them. Three demons in bladed armor crawl like spiders down the stairwell. One of them lifts her mask. It's Candiru.

"I told you what would happen if you hurt Lici," Candiru says.

"No, you don't understand," Jonathan says.

Candiru charges down the stairs and leaps at him.

Jonathan hits the gas on the motorcycle and flies across the workshop. Candiru goes over his head, barely nicking him on the shoulder with her bladed tail. Jonathan grabs his lego cell phone from the floor and sticks it to the side of his motorcycle. Then he turns around and goes for the door.

As he drives across the workshop, he feels the floor rumbling. Then Axlox crashes through the side of the lego house. The walls shatter. Legos rain down from the ceiling, sticking to the motorcycle. When the lego-covered ogre-sized demon swings, Jonathan ducks and rides out the front door. The house collapses like a tidal wave curling in on itself. Jonathan rides his motorcycle through the tube, into the street.

As Jonathan speeds down the block, he can hear the sound of five million pieces of lego coming down, avalanching into the street. The demons break out of the lego pile and chase after Jonathan as he heads toward the interstate.

It's rush hour traffic when Jonathan gets to the on-ramp, a long row of cars is backed up. Jonathan goes up the ramp, riding alongside the parked cars. The demons charge after him on all-fours, like cheetahs after their prey. As Jonathan passes a parked Prius, the driver does a double-take at the lego motorcycle riding by. He steps out of his car to get a better look. When Jonathan looks back at the guy, he sees Candiru coming up behind him. She whips her tail as she passes him, severing his head at the neck as well as his hand that was raised to block the sunlight from his eyes. The passengers in the other cars scream when they see it happen, but they stay in their seats.

The traffic is moving on the freeway when Jonathan gets on the road. He weaves between cars, trying to get away from the demons. Candiru climbs up on the back of a mustang. Then she leaps from car to car after Jonathan. The other demons follow. Way in the back, Jonathan sees Axlox. He punches cars out of the way as he runs down the road, rumbling the asphalt like a living earthquake.

Jonathan pulls his cell phone off the side of his motorcycle and calls Shoji.

"Shoji?" Jonathan yells into the phone as his sumo friend answers.

He can hardly hear Shoji's voice on the other end.

"Some Jesus freaks took Lici," Jonathan says. "They're going to kill her! You have to help me."

Shoji sounds alarmed on the other end.

"Go to Christ's Holy Church of Jesus," Jonathan says, and gives him the address. "I know it's a stupid name for a church, nevermind that now. Just get there before anything happens to her."

Then the phone cuts out. He tries sticking it back onto the motorcycle, but it pops right off the second he lets go. Lego pieces scatter across the freeway.

A cop on a motorcycle sees Jonathan driving like a maniac and pulls up beside him. He doesn't notice the demons coming up behind them.

"Pull over," the cop says, his lights flashing.

Jonathan points back at the demons closing in.

When the cop sees them, he faces forward. The cop speeds up, trying to escape just as much as Jonathan. He keeps the siren on, which causes the traffic ahead of them to pull over. Jonathan follows the cop down the freeway, toward the next exit.

As he looks back at the demons, Jonathan notices they are killing every human that gets in their path. All of the people pulling over in their cars are getting slashed with bladed tails as the demons pass. Blood sprays across the freeway. In the panic, cars crash into each other, horns blare, business men fly through windshields.

The cop points at Jonathan to take the next exit, but Jonathan has no intention of getting off the freeway yet. He still has a few exits to go. The cop changes lanes in front of him, pointing at a demon on Jonathan's tail. When Jonathan turns around, bladed claws slash toward him. The cop pulls out his gun and fires at the demon. Jonathan swerves and nearly crashes into the guardrail. A bullet hits the demon square in the chest and it falls under the wheels of a truck.

Jonathan separates from the cop as the officer takes the exit and goes down the ramp. But two demons go down the ramp after him. Before the cop goes out of sight, Jonathan sees a demon tail hooking him like a fish. His body flies off the back of the motorcycle, his spinal column and chunks of ribcage dangling out of his uniform.

Jonathan speeds up.

When Jonathan takes his exit, he looks back to see Candiru on his tail, but she's the only one. He dangerously speeds up going down the ramp, but there aren't any other cars to get in his way.

At the bottom of the ramp, he nearly hits a truck coming from the other direction. The driver slams on its breaks and holds down his horn as Jonathan rides safely around it. The truck cuts between Jonathan and Candiru, so the succubi queen leaps into the cab of the truck, crawls over the driver while shredding his torso with her claws, and leaps out of the driver's side window toward Jonathan. The truck driver cries out, still alive and holding his entrails as they spill between his legs.

Jonathan speeds up, trying to remember exactly how to get to the church. When he turns to see how close Candiru is getting, he sees her vanish from sight. When he looks forward, he sees her appear up ahead of him. She leaps into the air and lands on top of him feet-first. He flies off of the bike and hits the pavement. His bike continues on and crashes into a guardrail. The front of the vehicle explodes on impact, showering the street with legos.

Candiru lies on top of Jonathan, holding his arms down with her claws. His lower section is pinned down by her crotch. She slithers her tongue out at him, hissing like an angry snake. Her bladed tail points down at him like that of a scorpion's.

"Let me explain," Jonathan says.

Candiru strikes with her tail. The blade on the tip pierces the asphalt as Jonathan moves his head out of the way.

"I still love Lici," he says.

She strikes again, piercing the asphalt on the other side of his face.

"You don't even deserve to speak her name," says Candiru.

The tail strikes again, but this time Jonathan opens his mouth and bites it, just below the armor.

Candiru cries out and lifts him off of the ground, ready to rip his heart out with her claws.

"They're going to kill her," Jonathan says.

This makes Candiru pause.

"You have to believe me," Jonathan says. "A group of psychotic Christians led by my brother-in-law took her away. We have to save her. They plan to kill her and the baby."

"Where?" Candiru says.

"I'll bring you to her," Jonathan says.

Axlox and seven other demons arrive to them. Candiru looks over at her brother and says, "They have Lici. We have to stop them."

She drops Jonathan on the ground.

Jonathan says, "I care more about Lici than anyone else in

this world. We can't let anything happen to her."

When Axlox sees the genuine emotion in Jonathan's eyes, he looks angrily at his sister. "He doesn't look like someone who would have broken Lici's heart to me. I told you it was a mistake."

Candiru shrugs.

"Lici's groom could have been killed because of you," Axlox says, helping Jonathan to his feet. "She never would have forgiven us for that."

"I was mistaken," Candiru says.

Axlox looks down at Jonathan, blocking out the sun.

"Where is she?" he asks.

"We're close."

"Just think about the location," Axlox says, "and we'll be able to hone in on its position. We can teleport there."

Jonathan nods, then says, "Hold on."

He goes to his lego motorcycle and grabs the back half of it, that's still in one piece. Then he grabs a few handfuls of lego pieces and puts them into his pockets.

"Ready," Jonathan says.

Axlox places his hand on Jonathan's head, retrieving the location of the church. As the red ogre chants the teleportation spell, Jonathan begins constructing something new out of his living legos.

CHAPTER FOURTEEN

They appear outside of Christ's Holy Church of Jesus. Jonathan continues building a new lego device as he walks around the property.

"She's not in the church," Axlox says, smelling the air. "But she's close."

"Then she's in one of the other buildings," Jonathan says.

Jonathan knows that a lot of the money that Joseph's church makes goes into building extensions for the church. They've got basketball courts, a gym, a sauna, some apartments, a cafeteria, a community center, a private school, a kung fu dojo, a shooting range. It's not just a church, it's a compound.

They go to the largest building behind the church. There are two men outside.

"She's in there," Axlox says.

Jonathan holds them back.

"Wait a minute," Jonathan says. "Let me talk to them. If they'll let her go maybe nobody will get hurt."

"You have only one minute," Axlox says.

Standing in a basketball court outside the building, Jonathan calls out for his father. The demons stand in a row behind him. When the two guards outside see the demons, they rush inside.

"Don't hurt her," Jonathan yells, while working with the legos. "You're making a mistake."

When Jonathan's father steps to a window on the fourth floor, he has a cold look in his eyes.

"You're too late, Jonathan," his father says. One of the demons snickers when he hears the word jonathan.

"What do you mean?" Jonathan says.

"She's already dead."

Axlox puts his massive hand on Jonathan's shoulder.

"Don't worry," the ogre says. "He's lying. I can sense she's still alive up there."

"Look," Jonathan says. "If you don't release her people are going to die. These demons are her family. They're going to kill you."

Joseph peeks over his father's shoulder.

"No devil or demon can harm the Warriors of Jesus," Joseph says. "We have the power of the Lord on our side!"

"Trust me," Jonathan says. "You don't want to go to war with these demons. Just let Lici go. You have to let her live."

"We can't do that, son," his father says. "Demons are unholy creatures and we have to put a stop to them. We're doing God's work."

"Fuck God's work!"

His father goes silent. Jonathan can see Joseph and his father discussing something.

"It's not working," Candiru says. "We'll have to kill them."

Jonathan looks at her and says, "Can't you just teleport in there, grab her, and teleport back? Nobody has to get hurt."

"We can't," Axlox says. "We're on holy ground. We can't use our powers here."

"This is holy ground?" Jonathan says. "We're on a basketball court."

Jonathan's father comes back to the window.

"I'm sorry, Jonathan," his father says. "But we're going to have to kill you as well."

"What?" Jonathan thinks it has to be a joke.

"You've aligned yourself with unholy creatures from Hell," his father says. "You've obviously been corrupted by their evil. It's the only way to save your soul."

"You've got to be kidding me?" Jonathan says. "I'm your son."

Then he sees his mother and brother in the window. Both of them are covered in bandages.

"It's for the best," his mother says. "You'll thank me when we're in Heaven."

Jonathan hears a gun shot and a bullet hits the basketball court by his feet. He looks up to see a few men on the roof with rifles. They open fire on Jonathan. Axlox steps in front to act as a shield. When the bullets hit his flesh, they're only like bee stings to him.

"What the fuck?" Jonathan says, trying to finish his lego device. "They're actually trying to kill me."

"There's only one thing left to do," says Candiru. "We kill them all."

Jonathan nods.

"Fine," he says. "If you want a war you've got one."

Then Jonathan lifts the device in his arm. It is an enormous lego gatling gun. He aims it at the shooters on the roof and opens fire. Dozens of multi-colored bits of plastic shoot out, shredding the brick wall just below the shooters' heads. They duck for cover.

As smoke billows out the lego barrels of the homemade gatling gun, Jonathan rests it against his shoulder. Then he says, "Let's go."

The demons charge the building, with Jonathan close behind. They break down the door and slash through Christians on the other side. When Jonathan enters, he walks into a mess of meat and gore. Not a single corpse is left in tact as the demons release their fury on the men who kidnapped their beloved Lici.

As the demons go for the stairwell, three Christians with machine guns open fire. Two demons shriek as they are littered with bullets and fall to the ground. Axlox charges them, their bullets having no effect. With one punch, his fist hits two of them. Their bodies explode on impact like blood-filled water balloons on impact. The other keeps firing.

Candiru leaps over her brother's back and decapitates the gun man with her tail as she hits the steps. Then she darts up the stairs, tracking blood up the steps. Axlox breaks roof and ceiling outward so that he can fit through, and squeezes around the corner, up the stairs.

When they get to the second floor, the stairwell has been blocked off by furniture, forcing them to go into the second floor lobby. When they go through the door, they find themselves surrounded by the Warriors of Jesus. There are dozen of them, aiming rifles at their heads. The demons hold their ground. The Christians seem to be afraid to fire, shaking at the sight of them.

In one fast motion, Candiru jumps into Axlox's hand, he whips her in a circle, and tosses her over the Christians. She continues racing down the hallway. The Christians freeze, not moving an inch. Axlox and the other demons shove them out of the way and run down the hall after her. Jonathan remains in the circle, wondering why the Christians aren't moving. They just stand there with their guns pointed forward, unmoving.

As he waves his hand in front of one of them, the man blinks. Then the upper half of his body slides off and hits the guy standing next to him, and that guy's upper body falls in half. Like dominoes, the men fall into halves all around Jonathan. He jumps over their corpses and continues down the hall.

As Jonathan runs across the hallway, he sees several bodies flying through the air toward him. He ducks and corpses fly over his head. But when he looks back at them he realizes they aren't humans. They are demons. Their corpses have been pulverized, their chests caved in, as if a grenade had gone off. Jonathan continues down the hall and sees another demon corpse, shredded into pieces.

When he gets closer, he sees what's causing the destruction. There are three soldiers of God battling the demons at the end of the hall. They are not normal soldiers. They are more like cyborgs, with holy weaponry implanted into their flesh. Blasters implanted into their wrists shoot holy water at the demons. Crucifixes stick out of their arms and shoulders like spikes. They are wearing full plate armor, but instead of plates of steel they are armored with Jesus collector's plates from Christian Supply store. They are also armed with collectible Jesus battleaxes and war hammers.

One of the Jesus Cyborgs steps forward, an anti-demon bazooka folds out of his back onto his shoulder. Jonathan can see the Christian Supply logo on the side of the bazooka as it fires. The rocket that shoots out is actually a miniature porcelain Jesus-shaped cookie jar filled with holy water. It flies across the hallway and shatters against Axlox's crotch.

Axlox looks down as the holy water burns his penis.

"You hit me in the jonathan!" Axlox cries.

The entire floor rumbles as the ogre demon hits the ground.

The Jesus Cyborgs obliterate the rest of the demons, until it's just Jonathan left standing.

"Well," says one of the Jesus Cyborgs. "If it isn't the lego loser."

Jonathan recognizes that voice. The cyborg in the middle lifts

124

his Christian Supply helmet, revealing his face. Although he now has a laser eye, Jonathan recognizes that it is the freckled frat boy.

"Kill that demon-loving dickhead," says Freckled Frat Cyborg. The other two Jesus Cyborgs attack.

Jonathan raises his lego gatling gun and opens fire. The lego bullets shatter their Jesus collector's plate armor, sending bits of ceramic across the hall. The one with the bazooka on its shoulder launches a porcelain Jesus at him. Jonathan ducks and it shatters on the wall next to him. He runs at the cyborgs, firing his gatling gun. One of them falls back as multi-colored lego blocks pierce his chest. Blood sprays across the hall as he falls to the ground.

The other cyborg launches another porcelain Jesus. As Jonathan rolls out of the way, his lego gatling gun breaks against the floor. Another porcelain Jesus is fired and shatters on the ground next to the pile of legos.

Jonathan gets to his feet and pulls a lego shotgun out of his plaid suit. He pumps the lego bricks and fires. Several tiny single-pegged legos spray at the cyborg. The cyborg staggers back. Jonathan pumps and fires again. The cyborg staggers again as the blast hits him. Jonathan fires again, and again. As the Jesus Cyborg hits the ground, Jonathan lowers the barrel of his lego shotgun at the man's face and fires. Chunks of brain and lego pieces scatter across the floor.

"I'm coming for you, Lici," he says to himself, staring down at the man he just murdered. "I won't let anything get in my way."

Then Jonathan raises the gun to Freckled Frat Cyborg. When he pulls the trigger, it only clicks.

"What's wrong, lego loser?" says Freckled Frat Cyborg in a mock-baby voice. "Your little toy gun don't work no more?"

Jonathan realizes he's out of bullets. He takes apart the lego shotgun and tries to reconstruct it into a different weapon, as the frat boy comes toward him.

Freckled Frat Cyborg lifts his arm, the one that had been severed by Candiru in the bar the other night. It's now a weapon. Several razor-sharp metal crucifixes are sticking up out of what looks like the tip of a lance. When Freckled Frat Cyborg jerks his arm in the air like he's pumping a fist, an engine roars on his arm. The crucifixes whirl around the lance, like a drill.

Jonathan keeps working on his legos as fast as he can.

When Freckled Frat Cyborg attacks, Jonathan jumps out of the way. The drill cuts through the wall, shredding the drywall and stucco. As the frat boy tries to pull out his drill arm, Jonathan runs through blood and demon guts to the end of the hall. He puts his legos on a windowsill. Using both of his hands, Jonathan is able to work at full speed. Building so fast that his fingers become a blur, he puts the final pieces into place.

When Freckled Frat Cyborg reaches him, Jonathan turns around, revealing a lego chainsaw. It whirs to life. The frat boy swings his drill arm at the same time Jonathan swings the chainsaw. The weapons clash. As they hold their weapons together, bits of lego fly from the chainsaw and bits of metal fly from the crucifixes. The frat boy kicks Jonathan in the stomach and he falls back.

"I lost two of my frat brothers because of those demon assholes," says Freckled Frat Cyborg. "And without this arm I'll never be able to play football again."

The frat boy raises his other arm and a sword shoots out like a switchblade. On the side of the sword, there is a line of scripture Mark 16:17: In my name shall they cast out devils... On the other side of the blade, there's a web address for christiansupply.com with the slogan: Great savings, for those who have been saved!

"You're going to pay for what they did," says the frat boy, raising both the sword arm and drill arm into the air.

As the frat boy swings his sword, Jonathan lowers the chainsaw into his arm. The legos cut through his last arm, severing it at the elbow. The arm falls to the ground by his foot, still holding the sword. Blood sprays across the cyborg's Jesus collector's plate armor, as he screams.

Jonathan doesn't have enough time to block properly as the drill comes at him. It hits the center of the chainsaw, and legos fly into the air. The chainsaw falls apart in his hands, leaving him defenseless. Jonathan drops to the ground.

"You motherfucker!" cries Freckled Frat Cyborg, as he looks at his missing arm. "I'm going to cut you open and fill your guts with legos, demon-lover!"

The drill twists through the air toward Jonathan's face. Jonathan turns his head. Just as the drill cuts into Jonathan's hair, he feels the floor rumbling and hears something charging toward them.

"Leave Jonusan alone!" says the charging sumo.

When Jonathan looks back, he sees a large blubbery form slam into Freckled Frat Cyborg. The kid crashes through the window and shrieks all the way to the ground. Jonathan blinks. Shoji stands over him, drinking a can of Hamm's.

"I came as soon as I could, Jonusan," Shoji says, lifting him to his feet. "Crazy demon girlfriend in trouble?"

Jonathan nods and then realizes Shoji is mostly naked. He's dressed only in a yellow silk mawashi, the traditional sumo wrestling attire. However, he also has a six pack of Hamm's hanging from a strap on his waist. He pulls off one of the cans and offers it to Jonathan. Jonathan refuses, so Shoji two-fists the beers.

"She's upstairs," Jonathan says. "They're going to kill her."

"Then let's hurry, Jonusan," Shoji says with a drunken smile.

As Jonathan goes to the stairwell, he hears Axlox groaning down the hall.

Axlox says, "You have to save her. Don't let them get away with this."

Jonathan nods. The ogre tries to get to his feet, but just can't. The tendons in his thighs have melted away.

"I can see now that Lici has chosen a fine man to be her husband," Axlox says. "We have misjudged you."

Jonathan grabs a handful of broken legos and puts them in his pocket.

"I won't let anything happen to her."

Then Shoji and Jonathan head for the stairs.

In the stairwell, they step over dozens of dead Christians. Shoji nearly slips on the blood as they climb the stairs. They hear noise coming from above.

When they get up to the fourth floor, they see Candiru finishing off two more Jesus Cyborgs. She pulls her claws out of a man's guts and turns to Jonathan.

"Are you all that's left?" Candiru asks.

"Yeah," he says.

"Then let's go," she says. "Lici's close. I can sense it."

"She's still okay?" Jonathan asks.

"I don't know," says Candiru. "She's alive. That's all I know."

"We'll get her back," Jonathan says.

"We better," she says. "Or I'll hold you responsible. If it wasn't because of you none of this would have happened."

Jonathan decides to ignore the remark and lead them into the fourth floor hallway.

Jonathan, Candiru, and Shoji enter the church's kung fu dojo. Candiru points to the door on the other end of the room.

"She's through there," she says.

Standing in their way, however, is Joseph and his top five Christian martial arts students, all wearing silk uniforms. Joseph's uniform has white crosses on it.

"You've come far enough, Jonathan," Joseph says. "It's time you give up this foolishness."

"What and just allow you to kill me, my bride, and my unborn child?" Jonathan says. "Do you think I'm an idiot?"

"You don't understand the forces you're dealing with," Joseph says.

"You're the one who doesn't understand," Jonathan says. "I've seen the other side. I know your religion is just a sham. Lici is innocent. You're the real demons."

"Your mind has been corrupted," Joseph says. "I see there's no way to reason with you."

Joseph unleashes a battle cry which gets his students to their feet. He yells out again and the men attack.

Candiru charges the students. She rips one of their throats out, slices open one with her tail, claws another's stomach open. One of them spin-kicks her and she cuts both of his legs off, then snaps his neck. The last one she just grabs by the shoulders and chews his face off. She doesn't kill him. She just eats his facial flesh right off of his skull, while staring at Joseph on the far end of the room.

Joseph is angry when he hears his student's cries. He takes

a fighting stance, and flicks his hand at Candiru, daring her to come at him.

"Fight a real Warrior of God," Joseph says. "You foul witch."

Candiru drops the screaming student and wipes the blood from her mouth. She gets down on her knees and then lunges across the room at Joseph.

As she leaps into the air, she strikes with her tail. It comes at Joseph like a scorpion stinger. Joseph slaps her tail out of the air and kicks her in the stomach. She flies back across the room, surprised that he was able to touch her.

Candiru exposes her fangs and charges again. Joseph blocks her claw attacks, and then punches her in the throat. She staggers back. Her eyes glow red as she gets angry. She realizes Joseph hasn't even left the spot he's standing in.

When she comes at him again, Joseph gets serious. He kicks her in the thigh in midair, then punches her in the stomach. Her tail swipes at him, and he bends back to dodge. When he comes back up, he punches her in the face, knocking the red glow out of her eyes. But he doesn't stop there. He knees her in the stomach, punches her in the kidney. Then he jumps up in the air and elbows her in the skull so hard she flies across the room. When she hits the wall, her body collapses to the ground. Unconscious.

Joseph straightens his silk outfit and faces Jonathan.

"Evil can never defeat the power of God," Joseph says.

Jonathan didn't realize how good of a martial artist Joseph was. He knew he has been studying most of his life, but he's such a weasely-looking middle-aged douchebag that he couldn't believe he would have been so tough. He even defeated Candiru, the queen of the succubi.

"Surrender now, Jonathan," Joseph says. "Maybe I'll even spare your life. If you repent your sins and begin attending my sermons, perhaps we can rid you of the evil that corrupts your soul."

"I'll never surrender," Jonathan says. "I'll die before I let you kill Lici."

Joseph smiles and gets into a kung fu stance.

129

"I was hoping you would say that," he says.

Jonathan reaches into his pocket for his last handful of legos, but Shoji grabs him by the wrist.

Shoji looks Jonathan in the eyes and shakes his head.

"Jonusan, I will take care of this," says the sumo wrestler.

Shoji steps forward.

"A sumo?" Joseph says. "What do you possibly think you can do against me, fat ass?"

Shoji chugs a beer and tosses it aside.

"I have been learning Chinese Kung Fu since the age of seven," Joseph says. "I was the private disciple of Grand-Master Yip Wing Man of Choi Lee. I am proficient in Southern Shoulin, Tai Qi, Taekwondo, Inner Power Building Qi Gong, and Wing Chun."

Shoji ignores him. He squats down, bending his knees. He stomps his right foot, then his left foot.

Joseph continues, "I was the Champion of the 9th Hong Kong Annual Martial Arts Open Competition. I have trained in seven different countries. I have been ranked as the top martial artist in our state two years in a row. You have no idea who you are dealing with. I am the ultimate master of kung fu."

Shoji stomps two more times. He bends down, placing one hand on the mat in front of him, ready to lunge forward.

Then he says, "You fail to understand one thing."

"What's that?" Joseph says.

"Sumo destroys everything," Shoji says. "Even kung fu!"

Then Shoji charges him.

When Joseph sees the five hundred pound brick wall coming at him, his eyes widen. He jump-kicks Shoji, but it doesn't slow him down. Shoji's too drunk to feel anything. The sumo wrestler plows forward, ramming Joseph against the wall. Jonathan can hear a loud crunch on impact, as Joseph's leg is bent back over his head. Shoji continues shoving his weight into the kung fu expert, as he looks back at his friend.

"Go, Jonusan!" Shoji says. "Rescue your love!"

Jonathan crosses the room and takes the door on the other end.

"I'll finish him off," Shoji says.

Joseph screams in pain as his bones crack and bend against

the sumo's massive weight. He reaches out his hand to Jonathan, as if begging him for help, but Jonathan leaves him to his fate.

When Jonathan enters the room, he sees his father standing behind Lici with a knife to her throat. When Lici sees him, her eyes become wet. She shifts in her seat and smiles. Jonathan smiles back.

On the side of the room, Chuck and his mother lean against the wall. His mother looks like a mummy with all of the bandages covering her body.

Jonathan pulls the legos out of his pocket and quickly assembles a small handgun. He points it at his dad.

"Get away from her," Jonathan says, pointing the gun at his father.

When his dad sees the lego gun, he laughs.

"What the hell are you going to do with a lego gun?" his dad says.

Jonathan points it at the ceiling and fires. His family jumps.

"I'm not afraid to use it," Jonathan says.

"You can't shoot us," his father says. "We're your family."

"There's the family you're born into and the family you choose," Jonathan says. "You're not the family I chose."

His dad pulls the knife away and holds it in the air. He steps back.

"We were only trying to protect you, son," his father says.

"You were doing what you always do," Jonathan says. "You were imposing your will on me. You don't know what's best for me. You don't understand anything. You think I'm a loser. You think my fiancée is evil."

Jonathan steps forward and his father steps back.

"Well, you know what I think?" Jonathan says. "I think you're all the losers. I think you're all evil. Have you ever seen Lici do anything remotely evil? No. You just assume she is evil based on her race, and then you try to kill her. She's pregnant with your grandchild and you put a knife to her throat. Who do you think is the evil one here?"

His mother looks down at the floor.

Jonathan says, "Maybe demons are capable of committing evil, horrible acts, but no more than any human. If you knew what I knew about them, you'd realize they are also capable of love and goodness. They are no different than you or I."

Jonathan looks down at Lici.

"If you understood how much she means to me," he says to his family, though his eyes are on the demon girl, "how happy she makes me... " Jonathan takes her hand, folding her red fingers into his. "If you were to see the way she wags her tail when she plays the cello, the way she leaves me fire hearts across my bedroom floor, the way she smiles when she eats tiny frogs like chocolates, the way she pretends to like to play with legos just because she knows it makes me happy." Lici bites her lip piercing. "If you were to know her like I know her you'd see that she has one of the most beautiful souls of any being in this world, or the next. Maybe she is a demon from Hell, but I could never love a human half as much as I love her."

Lici jumps at Jonathan and wraps her arms around him, kissing him on his pale, trembling lips.

"My sweet Froggy... " she says, staring into him with her glowing green eyes.

As Jonathan lowers the lego gun, his father raises the knife and lunges at them.

"Get your hand off of him, demon!" his father cries.

Just as the tip of the knife is an inch from the demon's neck, the father's hand stops short. Jonathan and Lici turn around to see his bandaged, horribly burned mother clutching his father's wrist.

"Don't you dare hurt my future daughter-in-law," his mother says, tears running down her bandages. "You have no right."

Jonathan's father lets her pull the knife out of his hand. He looks at Jonathan, just for a second, and then breaks eye contact. He steps toward the back of the room.

"We made a mistake," Jonathan's mother says to Lici. "Please forgive us."

Lici nods at her.

"Of course I'll forgive you," Lici says to her. "We're family."

Then his mother wraps her bandaged arms around the demon, crying into her warm red skin.

As the family helps Lici through the doorway into the dojo, they see Shoji passed out in the middle of the room on top of Joseph. He's snoring loudly. Joseph is struggling to get out from under him, but he can't lift his massive weight.

When Joseph sees Lici he points at her and says, "Kill the demon! Kill her now!"

"We're not killing anyone," says the mother.

"She's corrupted you, too!" Joseph says. "She's bewitched you with her dark magic!"

"Shut the fuck up, Joseph," says the father.

Lici goes to the other side of the room and helps her sister to her feet.

"You're okay," Candiru says.

"My Froggy saved me," Lici says, pointing at Jonathan.

Jonathan smiles back at the succubus queen.

"Who defeated the priest?" Candiru asks.

As Jonathan helps the drunken sumo to his feet, he says, "Shoji did."

"Impressive," Candiru says.

When Shoji's eyes meet with Candiru's, they smile at each other and blush.

His mother claps her hands together.

"Well, if there's going to be a wedding tomorrow then we've got a lot of work to do," she says. "How about we all make plans over dinner?"

Everyone agrees.

As Chuck and his father try to lift Joseph's broken body, Jonathan goes to Lici and wraps his arm around her waist.

"We also have to make plans for a honeymoon," he says.

"Can it be in Hell?" she asks.

"Well... " Jonathan looks at the ceiling for a second. "That can be one option."

She kisses him on the neck and squeezes him against her belly. Jonathan smiles at her, trying to forget about all of the dead bodies scattered throughout the building.

CHAPTER FIFTEEN

Four years and a few days later, in a new lego house twice the size of the last one, Jonathan sets out a birthday cake on the dining room table. His entire family is there, singing happy birthday. His daughter, Cici, sits at the end of the table with a big smile on her face, her birthday hat lopsided on her head due to the tiny white horns peeking out from her long curly black hair. She has her father's blue eyes and her mother's smile. Her skin color is a bright shade of pink.

When the song is over, Cici says, "Can I blow them out now, mommy?"

Lici nods her head excitedly and Cici blows so hard that her tiny lizard tongue flickers out of her mouth like a kite tail.

After all the candles are out, the family cheers. Lici takes the cake and begins to cut it into slices with a knife on the end of her tail. With her hands, she holds her second child in one arm and her pregnant belly in the other.

"Come sit on grandma's lap," Jonathan's mother tells Cici, patting her thighs.

Cici smiles and jumps up into her grandma's lap.

"My, my," her grandma says to her in a giggling voice. "Your tail's getting so big!"

Cici kisses her grandma on her scarred cheek.

"People are going to think you're a monkey!" her grandma says.

"I'm not a monkey!" Cici says.

Her grandma tickles her belly. "You're a tickle monkey!"

Jonathan smiles as he sees his daughter laughing and screaming, trying to push away her grandma's tickling fingers.

Paige is standing next to her new husband, Mark. He's another devout Christian, but unlike Joseph he's actually a good man. He's a high school math teacher and doesn't own any of the tacky merchandise from Christian Supply.

Paige's daughter pulls on her mother's dress, begging her to build something with legos as good as the lego flower garden her uncle had made for her earlier in the day.

"I'm busy," Paige tells her daughter. "Why don't you go outside and play hide and seek with your cousin."

Her daughter says, "But she can teleport. It's no fair. She always wins."

"It's her birthday," Paige says. "She deserves to win."

Paige's daughter pouts and goes back to her uncle's legos.

Chuck and his new girlfriend drink a beer with his father. Chuck tries to talk sports, but his father can't stop talking about the architecture of Jonathan's new house. Even though it's made of legos, he still thinks it's an impressive design. He never did get to have the architect son he always wanted, but he thinks having a lego architect is the next best thing. Jonathan's dad flips the lights on and off. The electrical lighting really heightens the color of the legos.

"Here comes the famous lego artist now," his dad says as Jonathan steps toward them.

His dad clinks Jonathan's beer glass as he arrives.

"I saw the article on you in the Washington Post," his dad says. "I can't believe the president bought one of your sculptures for that much. It's ridiculous." He laughs and smacks Jonathan's shoulder. "I'm in the wrong business!"

Jonathan smiles and nods, then excuses himself as he hears a knock on the door.

When he opens the door, he sees Shoji standing there in a shiny new suit. Candiru stands next to him in a white evening gown, holding his hand.

"Jonusan!" Shoji says.

"Shoji!" Jonathan says.

They hug.

"Look, Jonusan!" Shoji says, grabbing Candiru's hand and shoving it into Jonathan's face. "Look! Look!"

Jonathan sees an engagement ring on Candiru's finger.

"I'm the happiest sumo in whole world!" Shoji says, as Candiru kisses him on the cheek with her blood-red lips.

"Congratulations," Jonathan says to both of them.

Shoji bows several times before he enters.

When Candiru shows Lici the ring, she says, "No way!" Then she jumps up in the air and hugs both Shoji and Candiru at the same time.

135

After the cake, Jonathan's mom pulls out the photos from the wedding.

"You looked so pretty in your wedding dress," his mother tells Lici.

They flip through the wedding photos. There's a picture of Lici's parents holding her hands, a picture of Axlox in the custom made suit, a picture of Uncle Xexus rolling down the aisle in his wheelchair, a picture of Joseph as he performs the ceremony with a terrified look on his face.

They hold the album open to a picture of Jonathan and Lici, kissing just after they were pronounced man and wife.

"Where am I?" Cici asks her mother.

Lici points at her pregnant belly in the photo.

"In here," she says. "You weren't born yet."

"You almost never were born," Chuck mumbles to himself. His father gives him an evil eye from across the table. Chuck should know they're never supposed to bring up those events ever again.

When Jonathan looks up from the photo, he sees that Lici is staring at him with a smile on her face and a tear in her eye.

"It almost didn't work out," Lici says to him.

Jonathan takes her hand and says, "No, but we made it work."

She kisses his hand as his daughter hugs his leg. Then Jonathan turns the page of the photo album to see what happened next.

ABOUT THE AUTHOR

Carlton Mellick III is one of the leading authors of the bizarro fiction subgenre. Since 2001, his books have drawn an international cult following despite the fact that they have been shunned by most libraries and chain bookstores.

He won the Wonderland Book Award for his novel, *Warrior Wolf Women of the Wasteland*, in 2009. His short fiction has appeared in *Vice Magazine, The Year's Best Fantasy and Horror #16, The Magazine of Bizarro Fiction,* and *Zombies: Encounters with the Hungry Dead*, among others. He is also a graduate of Clarion West, where he studied under the likes of Chuck Palahniuk, Connie Willis, and Cory Doctorow.

He lives in Portland, OR, the bizarro fiction mecca.

Visit him online at **www.carltonmellick.com**

Bizarro books

CATALOG   SPRING 2011

Bizarro Books publishes under the following imprints:

www.rawdogscreamingpress.com

www.eraserheadpress.com

www.afterbirthbooks.com

www.swallowdownpress.com

For all your Bizarro needs visit:

WWW.BIZARROCENTRAL.COM

Introduce yourselves to the bizarro fiction genre and all of its authors with the Bizarro Starter Kit series. Each volume features short novels and short stories by ten of the leading bizarro authors, designed to give you a perfect sampling of the genre for only $10.

BB-0X1
"The Bizarro Starter Kit"
(Orange)
Featuring D. Harlan Wilson, Carlton Mellick III, Jeremy Robert Johnson, Kevin L Donihe, Gina Ranalli, Andre Duza, Vincent W. Sakowski, Steve Beard, John Edward Lawson, and Bruce Taylor.
236 pages $10

BB-0X2
"The Bizarro Starter Kit"
(Blue)
Featuring Ray Fracalossy, Jeremy C. Shipp, Jordan Krall, Mykle Hansen, Andersen Prunty, Eckhard Gerdes, Bradley Sands, Steve Aylett, Christian TeBordo, and Tony Rauch. **244 pages $10**

BB-0X2
"The Bizarro Starter Kit"
(Purple)
Featuring Russell Edson, Athena Villaverde, David Agranoff, Matthew Revert, Andrew Goldfarb, Jeff Burk, Garrett Cook, Kris Saknussemm, Cody Goodfellow, and Cameron Pierce **264 pages $10**

BB-001"The Kafka Effekt" D. Harlan Wilson - A collection of forty-four irreal short stories loosely written in the vein of Franz Kafka, with more than a pinch of William S. Burroughs sprinkled on top. **211 pages $14**

BB-002 "Satan Burger" Carlton Mellick III - The cult novel that put Carlton Mellick III on the map ... Six punks get jobs at a fast food restaurant owned by the devil in a city violently overpopulated by surreal alien cultures. **236 pages $14**

BB-003 "Some Things Are Better Left Unplugged" Vincent Sakwoski - Join The Man and his Nemesis, the obese tabby, for a nightmare roller coaster ride into this postmodern fantasy. **152 pages $10**

BB-004 "Shall We Gather At the Garden?" Kevin L Donihe - Donihe's Debut novel. Midgets take over the world, The Church of Lionel Richie vs. The Church of the Byrds, plant porn and more! **244 pages $14**

BB-005 "Razor Wire Pubic Hair" Carlton Mellick III - A genderless humandildo is purchased by a razor dominatrix and brought into her nightmarish world of bizarre sex and mutilation. **176 pages $11**

BB-006 "Stranger on the Loose" D. Harlan Wilson - The fiction of Wilson's 2nd collection is planted in the soil of normalcy, but what grows out of that soil is a dark, witty, otherworldly jungle... **228 pages $14**

BB-007 "The Baby Jesus Butt Plug" Carlton Mellick III - Using clones of the Baby Jesus for anal sex will be the hip sex fetish of the future. **92 pages $10**

BB-008 "Fishyfleshed" Carlton Mellick III - The world of the past is an illogical flatland lacking in dimension and color, a sick-scape of crispy squid people wandering the desert for no apparent reason. **260 pages $14**

BB-009 **"Dead Bitch Army" Andre Duza** - Step into a world filled with racist teenagers, cannibals, 100 warped Uncle Sams, automobiles with razor-sharp teeth, living graffiti, and a pissed-off zombie bitch out for revenge. **344 pages $16**

BB-010 **"The Menstruating Mall" Carlton Mellick III** - "The Breakfast Club meets Chopping Mall as directed by David Lynch." - Brian Keene **212 pages $12**

BB-011 **"Angel Dust Apocalypse" Jeremy Robert Johnson** - Meth-heads, man-made monsters, and murderous Neo-Nazis. "Seriously amazing short stories..." - Chuck Palahniuk, author of Fight Club **184 pages $11**

BB-012 **"Ocean of Lard" Kevin L Donihe / Carlton Mellick III** - A parody of those old Choose Your Own Adventure kid's books about some very odd pirates sailing on a sea made of animal fat. **176 pages $12**

BB-015 **"Foop!" Chris Genoa** - Strange happenings are going on at Dactyl, Inc, the world's first and only time travel tourism company. "A surreal pie in the face!" - Christopher Moore **300 pages $14**

BB-020 **"Punk Land" Carlton Mellick III** - In the punk version of Heaven, the anarchist utopia is threatened by corporate fascism and only Goblin, Mortician's sperm, and a blue-mohawked female assassin named Shark Girl can stop them. **284 pages $15**

BB-021 **"Pseudo-City" D. Harlan Wilson** - Pseudo-City exposes what waits in the bathroom stall, under the manhole cover and in the corporate boardroom, all in a way that can only be described as mind-bogglingly irreal. **220 pages $16**

BB-023 **"Sex and Death In Television Town" Carlton Mellick III** - In the old west, a gang of hermaphrodite gunslingers take refuge from a demon plague in Telos: a town where its citizens have televisions instead of heads. **184 pages $12**

BB-027 **"Siren Promised" Jeremy Robert Johnson & Alan M Clark**
- Nominated for the Bram Stoker Award. A potent mix of bad drugs, bad dreams, brutal bad guys, and surreal/incredible art by Alan M. Clark. **190 pages $13**

BB-030 **"Grape City" Kevin L. Donihe** - More Donihe-style comedic bizarro about a demon named Charles who is forced to work a minimum wage job on Earth after Hell goes out of business. **108 pages $10**

BB-031**"Sea of the Patchwork Cats" Carlton Mellick III** - A quiet dreamlike tale set in the ashes of the human race. For Mellick enthusiasts who also adore The Twilight Zone. **112 pages $10**

BB-032 **"Extinction Journals" Jeremy Robert Johnson** - An uncanny voyage across a newly nuclear America where one man must confront the problems associated with loneliness, insane dieties, radiation, love, and an ever-evolving cockroach suit with a mind of its own. **104 pages $10**

BB-034 **"The Greatest Fucking Moment in Sports" Kevin L. Donihe**
- In the tradition of the surreal anti-sitcom Get A Life comes a tale of triumph and agape love from the master of comedic bizarro. **108 pages $10**

BB-035 **"The Troublesome Amputee" John Edward Lawson** - Disturbing verse from a man who truly believes nothing is sacred and intends to prove it. **104 pages $9**

BB-037 **"The Haunted Vagina" Carlton Mellick III** - It's difficult to love a woman whose vagina is a gateway to the world of the dead. **132 pages $10**

BB-042 **"Teeth and Tongue Landscape" Carlton Mellick III** - On a planet made out of meat, a socially-obsessive monophobic man tries to find his place amongst the strange creatures and communities that he comes across. **110 pages $10**

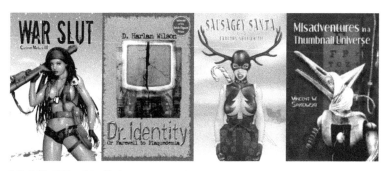

BB-043 **"War Slut" Carlton Mellick III** - Part "1984," part "Waiting for Godot," and part action horror video game adaptation of John Carpenter's "The Thing." **116 pages $10**

BB-045 **"Dr. Identity" D. Harlan Wilson** - Follow the Dystopian Duo on a killing spree of epic proportions through the irreal postcapitalist city of Bliptown where time ticks sideways, artificial Bug-Eyed Monsters punish citizens for consumer-capitalist lethargy, and ultraviolence is as essential as a daily multivitamin. **208 pages $15**

BB-047 **"Sausagey Santa" Carlton Mellick III** - A bizarro Christmas tale featuring Santa as a piratey mutant with a body made of sausages. 124 pages $10

BB-048 **"Misadventures in a Thumbnail Universe" Vincent Sakowski** - Dive deep into the surreal and satirical realms of neo-classical Blender Fiction, filled with television shoes and flesh-filled skies. **120 pages $10**

BB-049 **"Vacation" Jeremy C. Shipp** - Blueblood Bernard Johnson leaved his boring life behind to go on The Vacation, a year-long corporate sponsored odyssey. But instead of seeing the world, Bernard is captured by terrorists, becomes a key figure in secret drug wars, and, worse, doesn't once miss his secure American Dream. **160 pages $14**

BB-053 **"Ballad of a Slow Poisoner" Andrew Goldfarb** Millford Mutter-wurst sat down on a Tuesday to take his afternoon tea, and made the unpleasant discovery that his elbows were becoming flatter. **128 pages $10**

BB-055 **"Help! A Bear is Eating Me" Mykle Hansen** - The bizarro, heart-warming, magical tale of poor planning, hubris and severe blood loss...
150 pages $11

BB-056 **"Piecemeal June" Jordan Krall** - A man falls in love with a living sex doll, but with love comes danger when her creator comes after her with crab-squid assassins. **90 pages $9**

BB-058 **"The Overwhelming Urge" Andersen Prunty** - A collection of bizarro tales by Andersen Prunty. **150 pages $11**

BB-059 **"Adolf in Wonderland" Carlton Mellick III** - A dreamlike adventure that takes a young descendant of Adolf Hitler's design and sends him down the rabbit hole into a world of imperfection and disorder. **180 pages $11**

BB-061 **"Ultra Fuckers" Carlton Mellick III** - Absurdist suburban horror about a couple who enter an upper middle class gated community but can't find their way out. **108 pages $9**

BB-062 **"House of Houses" Kevin L. Donihe** - An odd man wants to marry his house. Unfortunately, all of the houses in the world collapse at the same time in the Great House Holocaust. Now he must travel to House Heaven to find his departed fiancee. **172 pages $11**

BB-064 **"Squid Pulp Blues" Jordan Krall** - In these three bizarro-noir novellas, the reader is thrown into a world of murderers, drugs made from squid parts, deformed gun-toting veterans, and a mischievous apocalyptic donkey. **204 pages $12**

BB-065 **"Jack and Mr. Grin" Andersen Prunty** - "When Mr. Grin calls you can hear a smile in his voice. Not a warm and friendly smile, but the kind that seizes your spine in fear. You don't need to pay your phone bill to hear it. That smile is in every line of Prunty's prose." - Tom Bradley. **208 pages $12**

BB-066 **"Cybernetrix" Carlton Mellick III** - What would you do if your normal everyday world was slowly mutating into the video game world from Tron? **212 pages $12**

BB-072 **"Zerostrata" Andersen Prunty** - Hansel Nothing lives in a tree house, suffers from memory loss, has a very eccentric family, and falls in love with a woman who runs naked through the woods every night. **144 pages $11**

BB-073 **"The Egg Man" Carlton Mellick III** - It is a world where humans reproduce like insects. Children are the property of corporations, and having an enormous ten-foot brain implanted into your skull is a grotesque sexual fetish. Mellick's industrial urban dystopia is one of his darkest and grittiest to date. **184 pages $11**

BB-074 **"Shark Hunting in Paradise Garden" Cameron Pierce** - A group of strange humanoid religious fanatics travel back in time to the Garden of Eden to discover it is invested with hundreds of giant flying maneating sharks. **150 pages $10**

BB-075 **"Apeshit" Carlton Mellick III** - Friday the 13th meets Visitor Q. Six hipster teens go to a cabin in the woods inhabited by a deformed killer. An incredibly fucked-up parody of B-horror movies with a bizarro slant. **192 pages $12**

BB-076 **"Fuckers of Everything on the Crazy Shitting Planet of the Vomit At smosphere" Mykle Hansen** - Three bizarro satires. Monster Cocks, Journey to the Center of Agnes Cuddlebottom, and Crazy Shitting Planet. **228 pages $12**

BB-077 **"The Kissing Bug" Daniel Scott Buck** - In the tradition of Roald Dahl, Tim Burton, and Edward Gorey, comes this bizarro anti-war children's story about a bohemian conenose kissing bug who falls in love with a human woman. **116 pages $10**

BB-078 **"MachoPoni" Lotus Rose** - It's My Little Pony... *Bizarro* style! A long time ago Poniworld was split in two. On one side of the Jagged Line is the Pastel Kingdom, a magical land of music, parties, and positivity. On the other side of the Jagged Line is Dark Kingdom inhabited by an army of undead ponies. **148 pages $11**

BB-079 **"The Faggiest Vampire" Carlton Mellick III** - A Roald Dahl-esque children's story about two faggy vampires who partake in a mustache competition to find out which one is truly the faggiest. **104 pages $10**

BB-080 **"Sky Tongues" Gina Ranalli** - The autobiography of Sky Tongues, the biracial hermaphrodite actress with tongues for fingers. Follow her strange life story as she rises from freak to fame. **204 pages $12**

BB-081 **"Washer Mouth" Kevin L. Donihe** - A washing machine becomes human and pursues his dream of meeting his favorite soap opera star. **244 pages $11**

BB-082 **"Shatnerquake" Jeff Burk** - All of the characters ever played by William Shatner are suddenly sucked into our world. Their mission: hunt down and destroy the real William Shatner. **100 pages $10**

BB-083 **"The Cannibals of Candyland" Carlton Mellick III** - There exists a race of cannibals that are made of candy. They live in an underground world made out of candy. One man has dedicated his life to killing them all. **170 pages $11**

BB-084 **"Slub Glub in the Weird World of the Weeping Willows" Andrew Goldfarb** - The charming tale of a blue glob named Slub Glub who helps the weeping willows whose tears are flooding the earth. There are also hyenas, ghosts, and a voodoo priest **100 pages $10**

BB-085 **"Super Fetus" Adam Pepper** - Try to abort this fetus and he'll kick your ass! **104 pages $10**

BB-086 **"Fistful of Feet" Jordan Krall** - A bizarro tribute to spaghetti westerns, featuring Cthulhu-worshipping Indians, a woman with four feet, a crazed gunman who is obsessed with sucking on candy, Syphilis-ridden mutants, sexually transmitted tattoos, and a house devoted to the freakiest fetishes. **228 pages $12**

BB-087 **"Ass Goblins of Auschwitz" Cameron Pierce** - It's Monty Python meets Nazi exploitation in a surreal nightmare as can only be imagined by Bizarro author Cameron Pierce. **104 pages $10**

BB-088 **"Silent Weapons for Quiet Wars" Cody Goodfellow** - "This is high-end psychological surrealist horror meets bottom-feeding low-life crime in a techno-thrilling science fiction world full of Lovecraft and magic..." -John Skipp **212 pages $12**

BB-089 "Warrior Wolf Women of the Wasteland" Carlton Mellick III
Road Warrior Werewolves versus McDonaldland Mutants...post-apocalyptic fiction has never been quite like this. **316 pages $13**

BB-090 "Cursed" Jeremy C Shipp - The story of a group of characters who believe they are cursed and attempt to figure out who cursed them and why. A tale of stylish absurdism and suspenseful horror. **218 pages $15**

BB-091 "Super Giant Monster Time" Jeff Burk - A tribute to choose your own adventures and Godzilla movies. Will you escape the giant monsters that are rampaging the fuck out of your city and shit? Or will you join the mob of alien-controlled punk rockers causing chaos in the streets? What happens next depends on you. **188 pages $12**

BB-092 "Perfect Union" Cody Goodfellow - "Cronenberg's THE FLY on a grand scale: human/insect gene-spliced body horror, where the human hive politics are as shocking as the gore." -John Skipp. **272 pages $13**

BB-093 "Sunset with a Beard" Carlton Mellick III - 14 stories of surreal science fiction. **200 pages $12**

BB-094 "My Fake War" Andersen Prunty - The absurd tale of an unlikely soldier forced to fight a war that, quite possibly, does not exist. It's Rambo meets Waiting for Godot in this subversive satire of American values and the scope of the human imagination. **128 pages $11**

BB-095 "Lost in Cat Brain Land" Cameron Pierce - Sad stories from a surreal world. A fascist mustache, the ghost of Franz Kafka, a desert inside a dead cat. Primordial entities mourn the death of their child. The desperate serve tea to mysterious creatures. A hopeless romantic falls in love with a pterodactyl. And much more. **152 pages $11**

BB-096 "The Kobold Wizard's Dildo of Enlightenment +2" Carlton Mellick III - A Dungeons and Dragons parody about a group of people who learn they are only made up characters in an AD&D campaign and must find a way to resist their nerdy teenaged players and retarded dungeon master in order to survive. 232 **pages $12**

BB-097 **"My Heart Said No, but the Camera Crew Said Yes!" Bradley Sands** - A collection of short stories that are crammed with the delightfully odd and the scurrilously silly. **140 pages $13**

BB-098 **"A Hundred Horrible Sorrows of Ogner Stump" Andrew Goldfarb** - Goldfarb's acclaimed comic series. A magical and weird journey into the horrors of everyday life. **164 pages $11**

BB-099 **"Pickled Apocalypse of Pancake Island" Cameron Pierce** A demented fairy tale about a pickle, a pancake, and the apocalypse. **102 pages $8**

BB-100 **"Slag Attack" Andersen Prunty** - Slag Attack features four visceral, noir stories about the living, crawling apocalypse. A slag is what survivors are calling the slug-like maggots raining from the sky, burrowing inside people, and hollowing out their flesh and their sanity. **148 pages $11**

BB-101 **"Slaughterhouse High" Robert Devereaux** - A place where schools are built with secret passageways, rebellious teens get zippers installed in their mouths and genitals, and once a year, on that special night, one couple is slaughtered and the bits of their bodies are kept as souvenirs. **304 pages $13**

BB-102 **"The Emerald Burrito of Oz" John Skipp & Marc Levinthal** OZ IS REAL! Magic is real! The gate is really in Kansas! And America is finally allowing Earth tourists to visit this weird-ass, mysterious land. But when Gene of Los Angeles heads off for summer vacation in the Emerald City, little does he know that a war is brewing...a war that could destroy both worlds. **280 pages $13**

BB-103 **"The Vegan Revolution... with Zombies" David Agranoff** When there's no more meat in hell, the vegans will walk the earth. **160 pages $11**

BB-104 **"The Flappy Parts" Kevin L Donihe** - Poems about bunnies, LSD, and police abuse. You know, things that matter. 132 **pages $11**

BB-105 **"Sorry I Ruined Your Orgy" Bradley Sands** - Bizarro humorist Bradley Sands returns with one of the strangest, most hilarious collections of the year. **130 pages $11**

BB-106 **"Mr. Magic Realism" Bruce Taylor** - Like Golden Age science fiction comics written by Freud, *Mr. Magic Realism* is a strange, insightful adventure that spans the furthest reaches of the galaxy, exploring the hidden caverns in the hearts and minds of men, women, aliens, and biomechanical cats. **152 pages $11**

BB-107 **"Zombies and Shit" Carlton Mellick III** - "Battle Royale" meets "Return of the Living Dead." Mellick's bizarro tribute to the zombie genre. **308 pages $13**

BB-108 **"The Cannibal's Guide to Ethical Living" Mykle Hansen** - Over a five star French meal of fine wine, organic vegetables and human flesh, a lunatic delivers a witty, chilling, disturbingly sane argument in favor of eating the rich.. **184 pages $11**

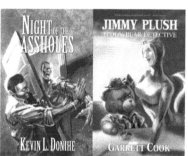

BB-109 **"Starfish Girl" Athena Villaverde** - In a post-apocalyptic underwater dome society, a girl with a starfish growing from her head and an assassin with sea anenome hair are on the run from a gang of mutant fish men. **160 pages $11**

BB-110 **"Lick Your Neighbor" Chris Genoa** - Mutant ninjas, a talking whale, kung fu masters, maniacal pilgrims, and an alcoholic clown populate Chris Genoa's surreal, darkly comical and unnerving reimagining of the first Thanksgiving. **303 pages $13**

BB-111 **"Night of the Assholes" Kevin L. Donihe** - A plague of assholes is infecting the countryside. Normal everyday people are transforming into jerks, snobs, dicks, and douchebags. And they all have only one purpose: to make your life a living hell.. **192 pages $11**

BB-112 **"Jimmy Plush, Teddy Bear Detective" Garrett Cook** - Hardboiled cases of a private detective trapped within a teddy bear body. **180 pages $11**

9 781936 383825